DATE	BORROWER'S NAME	

'87

'87

'87

© THE BAKER & TAYLOR CO.

The MAN
in the
IRON MASK

P. HOYLE

The MAN
in the
IRON MASK

CARCANET

First published in the United States of America in 1986 by
Carcanet Press Limited
198 Sixth Avenue, New York, NY 10013

British Library Cataloguing in Publication Data

  Hoyle, Peter
    The man in the iron mask.
    I. Title
    823′.914[F]   PR6058.09/

    ISBN 0-85635-659-X pb
    ISBN 0-85635-499-6 hb

Typeset by Paragon Photoset, Aylesbury
Printed in England by SRP Ltd, Exeter

To Barbara
with love

I

CHAPTER ONE

*Monsieur d'Artagnan will
conduct the prisoner to the Ile
Sainte-Marguerite. He will cover his face
with an iron visor, which the prisoner
cannot raise without peril to his life.*
The Vicomte de Bragelonne   ALEXANDER DUMAS

For six months in the flat immediately above mine lived the recluse who believed himself to be the Man in the Iron Mask. Although an invincible shyness prevented him making contact with anyone else in the block, he made an exception for me under the impression that I was his gaoler, Saint-Mars, or his enemy d'Artagnan. When he was in a mood for talking he would constantly recall his experiences in the Bastille or the fortress of Sainte-Marguerite.

His flat was sparsely furnished. In the one room that he used, there was a card-table, a chair, a stool, a chest of drawers, a bed-settee. I wondered if the large portmanteau in one of the other virtually empty rooms contained books. A total absence (with one exception in the entrance-hall) of ornaments, pictures, and mirrors.

Absorbed in writing his memoirs, he used to sit at the card-table pushed right up to a rear window. Not many yards away he had a view of the brick wall of a derelict mill which bore the faded slogan: *Half the Male Population of this District is wearing Cash and Co's Hats.* Occasionally he complained that this curtain wall of Richelieu's fortress obscured his view of the sea.

At first, if he was working when I visited him, he would hastily cover his manuscript with a duster. Later I saw that beneath a protective sheet of stiff card studded with black beetles intended to be fleur-de-lis, the title THE MAN IN THE IRON MASK, in great swash letters, filled nearly two-thirds of his first page. The recluse used to point out to me that the huge solidly printed black letters of this sinister title could simultaneously represent the grid of a sarrasin or portcullis, the grating of an oubliette, the grilled window of a cell, or — more important — the close set bars of the umbril itself, prison within a prison, locked above the prisoner's shoulders.

At no time did I see the recluse wear an iron mask, or a mask of any kind, neither black velvet, nor cheap cloth, nor even cardboard. On the one occasion that I mentioned this (approaching the topic with care because he could be unpredictable in his temper if something was said that upset him) he nodded and muttered, only just audibly, what I took to be 'Special dispensation'.

From random remarks he made I gathered that he believed his arch-enemy, the King, to be in his dotage. He himself was, without question, still the chief state prisoner of the land, with no possibility of ever being permitted his freedom, but over the years he had become no more than a vague memory to the few survivors who were originally a party to the secret, and consequently the severe conditions of his imprisonment had been gradually relaxed. About the statuesque Queen, his mother (whom he appeared to know to be dead), his feelings were mixed. At times he was sentimental and spoke of her ageless marmoreal beauty. At other times, overcome by the thought of the Queen's monstrous cruelty to him, he gloated over the breast cancer that had killed her, as a fitting retribution.

Because he was such an inoffensive neighbour I was anxious that no one inform the authorities of his eccentricities. The contrast between the royal prisoner and the fiends who lived below me was marked. I would have regarded it as an ideal state of affairs if the entire block had been occupied by quiet madmen like the recluse. In Ruskin House unbearable noise was the norm, any treacherous lull merely a refinement of torture.

At all hours footballs pounded the decorative windbreaks in the forecourt and the wall of the derelict mill round the back; on summer evenings teenage motorcyclists used the echoing blood-red canyons between our block and the next as a speedway circuit. By contrast the flat of the Man in the Iron Mask was a refuge. Whenever I crossed the threshold, tranquillity seemed to emanate from the hunched figure in the back room. I noticed a patient melancholy smile if he did become aware of the drum-fire outside; sometimes I fancied he believed that what he heard was the fury of a stormy sea, the breakers exploding against the rocks of Ile Sainte-Marguerite, or, perhaps, the groundswell of Revolution carried through the thickness of the Bastille's walls. There would be no hope in his eyes as he listened, head cocked on one side.

One day, however, perhaps a couple of months after I got to know him and about the time that I first considered writing the notes that developed into this narrative, I was greeted differently when I entered the recluse's room. He looked round at me alertly, smiled, and nodded, his lank silver-streaked hair falling down over his normally unfocused eyes.

'I expected you today, Monsieur,' he said. 'I know you bring a message from the King.'

'No, Monseigneur,' I replied. 'I am no messenger. Surely you recognize me. I am your friend.'

He started gnawing the end of his pen, his gaze fixed on the grimy window.

'Understand that I am an enemy of the musketeers, and you above all, d'Artagnan!' he said.

Then he took a pack of cards from his dressing-gown pocket and resumed speaking as he spread them in a horseshoe over his manuscript.

'Those crutched friars in their heralds' tabards are mere playing-cards to me,' he said. 'Here comes the Two of Swords! Here comes the vainglorious Chevalier of Swords! But Old Poitrine, the faithful sentry, with his partisan . . . [here he gestured with his pen] Old Poitrine sweeps them back, sweeps them aside, sweeps them away. I will brook no resistance, Monsieur.' Matching his actions to his words, he scattered all the cards on the floor, followed by the pages of his manuscript and even his biro-and-quill pen.

'I have kept silence all my life,' he concluded grandiloquently. 'Now I will take vengeance on the whole world.'

Then he burst into tears. I decided to leave, and shut the door on the landing very gently. Back in my own flat I could hear a woman's voice raised in anger downstairs, but no sound from the flat above. Not long afterwards I returned to make him a hot drink, hoping that by then he would be more composed. To my surprise, when I took the tea in to him, the playing-cards had been gathered up and the manuscript was back on the card-table covered by its dingy cloth. He was stretched out on his old grey couch, asleep.

From the third or fourth week of our acquaintance, as well as making notes on my neighbour, I had got into the habit of rehearsing for my role of confidant by re-reading the d'Artagnan romances. As it happened, among the oldest volumes on my shelves was an anonymous translation of *Le Vicomte de Bragelonne*. Stretched out on the camp bed that I had bought after my wife left me, I would read avidly and at great speed the worldly fairytales of d'Artagnan, his friends, enemies and masters. From my position close to the evil-smelling floor, nothing was visible of the flats and the outside world except the sky. At this time I was particularly subject to migraine attacks, perhaps caused by the constant tension of those torture-by-hope silences, of dreading the moment when a fresh commotion outside would destroy my fugitive peace.

The first symptoms would be the floaters, smoke-lariats and zigzags coming between me and the page. Later I would imagine I could see megaliths or basalt columns, like fragments from the Giant's Causeway or Fingal's Cave, or perhaps the Grotto of Locmaria, the mass of boulders entombing the remains of Porthos.

CHAPTER TWO

*'Call me neither Monsieur nor
Monseigneur! Call me ACCURSED!'*

Early in our relationship I developed a biography for my neighbour, an outline of the growth of his mania, before I was in
possession of even the most basic facts. For a long time my only
demonstrable error lay in assuming he had been unhappily
married and that this had contributed to his obsession. The
transference from my own situation, I am afraid, is all too
obvious.

Concerning the legend of the Man in the Iron Mask, I had
read Dumas. I had also read one or two popular accounts of the
mystery of the masked prisoner. My own crude explanation was
that the prisoner was the King's bogeyman, kept on hand to
frighten the few noblemen unimpressed by the threat of banish-
ment to their estates. The man wearing the mask was a relative
nonentity, unaware of the reason why he was acting out a cruel
and tedious charade. Thus two actors, 'fantastical monarcho'
and grizzled gaoler, spent a lifetime yawning at each other
across a chess-board.

I imagined that my neighbour's real life had been spent more
or less continuously like my own beneath a minus sign. With
Rousseau he could have said that his worst faults had been
those of omission: crucial appointments he had never intended
to keep, character-building challenges he had ignored, knacks
he had been certain he could never master — a life of deliberate
evasions. These omissions and evasions, these deliberate re-
nunciations were central to my idea of his character. Fear of
ridicule, fear of exposing himself to censure or laughter, had
dominated this man's life.

And yet although apparently so lacking in spirit and initiative the unfortunate man could not eradicate an irrational
sense of superiority. It was this mixture of abasement and pride
that compelled him to enter an imaginary world peopled and

furnished out of his reading until gradually he came to identify himself with one semi-legendary character.

I could see how essential it was for the sake of his imaginative projections for him to live the life of a recluse — recluse, that is rather than convict. The solitary confinement of the 'ancient, tranquil' prisoner in his island fortress had many affinities with the lives of those saintly recluses of rarest distinction, the hermits of the early Church, isolated in the desert, in caves, or on off-shore rocky islets.

As long as he felt that his exceptional position was recognized, it seems likely that this state of simulated incarceration was something my neighbour had a positive liking for. The more obvious the constraints, the more complete the identification. The topography of Fort Réal would be a diagram of felicity for him. Even the prospect of the smaller and darker confines of the Bastille cell at the end of his life may have afforded him some perverse satisfaction.

Even squalor may have seemed romantic to him as long as some vestige of nobility remained, as long as he could regard himself as one specially marked for an exceptional misfortune. ('That isolation for forty years confined within walls of stone and iron.')

I imagined that long before his fantasies had crystallized around the legend of the unknown prisoner, my neighbour had acquired a fondness for the grand gesture and patrician speech, a special language for kings and poets. In *his* case, of course, the chosen role, the lofty utterance, were to be exclusively concerned with the acceptance of a great misfortune, of exile, abdication, imprisonment, and death, acted out with appropriately regal dignity.

The monotony of the victim's role never palled on him. Keeping pace with the growth of his obsession, he refined his technique in isolation. (The wife I had invented for him, who borrowed her features from my own estranged wife, must, I thought, have left him.) As his knowledge of his role grew, and his performance matured, the technique of his double vision grew ever more efficient. The translation from reality to dream-world was effected instantaneously, with supreme confidence.

No awkward fumbling for an approximate equivalent, but a clear comprehensive vision of what was not there or at least what was invisible to other eyes, at every moment of the day.

I am sure that, as far as he was concerned, the fairytale aspect never jarred with elements that were prosaic and circumstantial.

From the very beginning I had noticed how effortless the trick of transformation had become for him. It was second nature to him to utilize the simplest objects, the most banal activity, in the construction of flights of fantasy. Even something as trifling as a margin ruled straight, and then, his hand jerking, goose-stepping out at an angle, became a talus, a bold slope at the base of a tower which he gazed at fascinated, pen in hand, while he elucidated its purpose in the art of fortification.

Did I know, he once asked me, that his nickname was 'The Tower'? And did I know, he added with an ironic smile, that in the King's communications to his Minister, he, Philippe of the House of Bourbon, elder brother to that other Philippe, the degenerate Duke of Orleans, was always Eustache Dauger?

I run ahead of my story: let me return to the beginning. It was shortly before Easter when he arrived, though unknown to me for at least a fortnight. Even for March the weather was severe, but this did not deter the children of the flats from pounding the windbreaks with their footballs, from delighting in their hellish uproar.

The barking dogs I preferred to the noisy children. Perhaps this will sound childish but I gave the dogs names such as Eager Dog, Limper, and Trembler (a dog whose hindquarters were always aquiver). My favourite was Cringer — a skeletal, dingy, black old dog (abject when not actually cowering) who had a melancholy head, and frost on his eyebrows. It was only very occasionally — red-letter days or rather hours — that the forecourt was silent, empty of both dogs and children.

No sound issued from within the upstairs flat. The silence would have been absolute if the outer walls had been the required dungeon thickness.

My neighbour was a madman to most of the occupants of the block simply because he was a recluse. As far as I could tell, no one but myself knew the extent of his *éloignement* from the lives of the old people, the problem families, the one-parent families, the immigrants, and others who made up the population of Ruskin House. Sequestered in his third-floor flat, gazing for hours, pen in hand, at the hieroglyphics on the monstrous wall, perceiving no real face, hearing no real voice, my neighbour was 'cut off by an immeasurable gulf from the ordinary tide and succession of human affairs'. Almost certainly, no one other than myself knew he believed himself to be the unhappy twin of Louis XIV.

If I forget and on occasion call him 'madman' myself, I mean no disrespect. It is a matter of taste I suppose. I prefer a muted life spent in half-lights, in a minor key. My neighbour's company was therapeutic to me. He scribbled. He was quiet. His frail appearance was almost kingly. I could practically guarantee that an afternoon spent in his company would be peaceful.

However I had to be careful to adopt the right attitude; not to be too casual and relaxed, that is, not to be slack, unbuttoned, in a present-day state of mind, and not to be (on the other hand) in a tense, sceptical, clinical state of mind, thinking of my neighbour merely as a bizarre case history. Above all I had to remember to be dignified, formal and deferential in my manner. Here I am at a definite advantage. I find it easy to be valet-like, to defer to the more dominant, more decisive personality.

When I arrived the recluse would give only the slightest indication that he had noticed my presence. Usually this didn't involve any interruption in the progress of his scribbling. Until he noticed me I didn't venture across the threshold. If I found myself hovering too long for comfort (I always want to urinate if I stand for any length of time in one spot) I gave a deferential cough.

I think it helped me, too, in adopting an artificial old-fashioned mode of discourse, that I have no natural idiomatic way of speaking (or writing). A teacher once told me that I wrote 'a kind of police-report English' in which people never 'eat' but 'partake of refreshment'. It is true that the archaic (even recondite) and stilted expression comes naturally to me. In fact when I use a local phrase, people tend to look at me askance as though I had spoken Chinese. (This may have something to do with my enunciation and doubtful audibility.) Looking back it is difficult to explain my attachment to the recluse, the reasons why I took such pains to minister to his illusions, except that to some extent I must have taken pleasure in acting the part of the irreproachable Brooksmith to this proud pariah. I also had almost unlimited free time, and nothing to do other than dwell on my migraine and various other minor disorders.

There was little that was arduous in my duties. I brought him food, but I had to get food for myself anyway. I did a little dusting but only in his study-bedroom. I took his washing to the laundrette. But what I remember most is watching him write and striving to make a suitable rejoinder when he spoke. Much of what he later referred to as information I had fed him in the past was entirely his own invention, or remembered from his reading. To hear him talk you would have thought I was as knowledgeable as the King's private secretary and had given him a regular digest of information on all court matters of the later seventeenth century. My role then was partly that of home help but chiefly that of confidant, except that, I should say, I was several confidants in one, by turns Prison Governor, Bénigne de Saint-Mars, Aramis and d'Artagnan. Sometimes I was treated as an honoured near-equal. Sometimes I was treated very much as an inferior. Usually I was cast in a fairly sympathetic role but there were times when I was treated with deep suspicion. It is true, as I have already mentioned more than once, that the Man in the Iron Mask was a gentle madman. Nevertheless he was capable, at least from time to time, of convincing impersonations of a sovereign's displeasure (or Pretender's tantrums).

CHAPTER THREE

*The age of the curled, daredevil swash-
buckler with his Gascon flourish and
moustache en croc, who wore at all times a
stout pistol-proof, dagger-proof cuirass
beneath his casaque.*

In the recluse's narrow entrance hall (alike in all the flats) were
two roundels, not framed but sellotaped to the chipboard
brown wallpaper. The top picture, entitled THE WOUNDED
MUSKETEER — ATHOS, and apparently a reproduction of
a nineteenth-century lithograph, showed the wounded Athos
asleep in 'the worst inn's worst room', his head propped up
against the bolster, an aristocratic haughty countenance,
hollow cheeks, curled disdainful lip, nose aquiline and shaving-
thin, heavy-lidded eyes (closed), silvery goatee (uncombed),
lank hair (dishevelled) . . .

In this roundel the wounded Count wore a lace-fronted
nightshirt, his sword arm (bandaged) lay across his breast.
There was a flimsy barricade of furniture against the door in
case the robbers, assassins or Cardinal's guards returned to
administer the *coup de grâce*. His ancestral sword, the weapon
with the magnificent swept hilt so often admired by Porthos in
the rue Ferronnière, lay on the floor attached to a discarded
sword-belt. A breastplate leaned against the wall beneath a
gigantic spider's web. Empty bottles, a flagon, a dice-box and
playing-cards littered the marble slab of a commode. On a
prie-dieu near the canopied bed the silver butts of two horse-
pistols were within easy reach.

Everything about Athos in the picture reminded me of my
neighbour, but I would not press the reality of the resemblance
and I freely admit that he resembled portraits of Charles I
more. The haughty expression, the pallor, the weary but still
seignorial bearing, the slender be-ringed fingers of his left hand
that had perhaps just ceased to fidget with the coverlet — all
suggested to me interminable sickbed afternoons in a haggard

light, lonely afternoons during which, relieved only by fugitive intervals of oblivion (dreamwisps merely), the invalid was forced to endure the clacking of the halyard against the flag-pole, the noise of bandogs tenting, a malt-horse or courier's post-horse stamping briefly on the cobbles, the protracted speculative cackling of hens (like a question under numerous heads, with an indecisive interminable reply) or, more distant, noises of hammering or sawing or children at play, remote noises, or, closer at hand again, the scrannel piping of birds under the eaves above the open galleries of the rambling dilapidated hostelry — of all the sounds surely the most weari-some — their faint hopeless mocking glissandos.

At the window, unseen by the invalid Chevalier, (unnoticed by me the first half-dozen times I looked at the picture but the lobby of course was dark, the wallpaper sombre) was a swarthy man with a melon grin under a broad feathered hat, a rotonde round his neck, wearing a dark uniform with a moline cross at the shoulder, a dagger with a rouelle guard in his hand. The Count looked so weak the hoariest bang-beggar might get the upper hand of him.

In the companion lithograph beneath, the intruder, the villainous Reformado, swivel-eyed and smiling like a zany, was advancing towards the bed. Unaccountably, in this second picture, it was no longer afternooon but vesper-time. A tallow candle had appeared among the other items on the marble slab. A magnified shadow darkened the back wall (on which a crucifix was just visible), a shadow of the assassin and the point of the misericord descending . . .

I was almost sure there was no basis in Dumas for the scenes thus depicted. I knew that Athos died of a broken heart caused by the death of his too perfect son, Raoul. The only assassination that took place in an inn was when Miladi's son Mordaunt stabbed his mother's executioner. And yet could I be sure that such an episode did not occur? I have always found those rapid, umbratile, ramshackle books fade from the memory amazingly quickly no matter how often you re-read them.*

*Author's note: I will read *The Vicomte* again. I may have missed something. Bored by the tedious imbroglios of an uninspired collaborator I may have

The artistry of the pictures was certainly very fine. There was no signature apparently. I examined them almost every time I called on my neighbour. It became something of a ritual like adjusting and readjusting the barometer in the entrance hall of my own flat. Evidently the pictures had some connection with his obsession but I never dared broach the subject with him.

At any rate, the two roundels were not figments of my imagination. The Rent Collector examined them too. The day he came to the door asking about my neighbour upstairs I was confused, uncertain what to do for the best. I was further confused by the name in the rent book — MARCHIALI. Half in a dream I followed the official up the flight of dusty concrete steps to the next landing where I pressed the bell twice and then pretended to recollect that I had a key and that my neighbour was hard of hearing. (At any rate I muttered something to that effect. I made some pretence at an explanation, used a mild expletive perhaps.)

As soon as I had got the door open, the Rent Collector went up to the sellotaped pictures. He smiled at them. Behind his spectacles his bulging kindly eyes looked enormous. He was swarthy, had pepper-and-salt curly hair. He looked Italian or mulatto.

'One for all and all for one,' he said with a northern accent.

'Marchiali' in the back room was asleep on his couch. I opened his door, closed it quickly. The Rent Collector looked round the dirty living-room.

'He is a shift-worker,' I told the official. 'I think it will be best if he leaves the money with me when you call in future.'

The man seemed satisfied enough with this arrangement but kept looking back at the curtainless window, at the cobwebs festooning the ceiling and the empty corner where, in any other flat, a TV set would have been standing. The expression on his face was one of unease — part wonderment, part distaste.

Going back downstairs I met my estranged wife Brenda and her West Indian friend on their way up to a flat on the fourth

skipped the odd chapter here and there. In *The Memoirs of d'Artagnan* a lustful rather than noble Athos almost dies of his wounds because he will not discontinue love-making with his mistress.

floor. She gave a brief thrusting look ('her keen glance a stiletto which pierces every cuirass') after my stammered greeting. Hearing a gulp of laughter when she was a flight above me, I looked up and glimpsed her shiny red high-heeled boots through the dusty blue-painted railings. The man, following her at a more leisurely pace, smiled down at me over the banisters, showing gleaming white teeth.

Two hours later I heard footsteps descending from the fourth floor, and laughter. A noise like a bull charging the railings. The reverberations died away gradually. The heavy double outer doors slammed. Then I heard Brenda, in the open air, calling my name with a heavy sneer.

Obviously tipsy she was standing at the edge of the threadbare, sloping lawn, shouting up abuse at my window. In the distance I was vaguely aware of the handsome slim West Indian in conversation with a man on crutches, a notorious womanizer who had received his injuries leaping from a fat blonde's bedroom window the night her husband returned — 'stopped short in their transports as if struck by a blow from a club'.

Suddenly Brenda screamed, half turned, slipped and fell on to her back. She got up quickly, her camel coat daubed with mud, perhaps also with dog dirt, and ran off towards her friend who was still engrossed in conversation with the man on crutches.

No doubt because of this unpleasantness, one of my headaches started. I drew the curtains although it was still daylight and sank down on to the camp bed safely hidden from Brenda and the world. Some time later when I woke it was dark. The curtains didn't quite meet. On the ceiling an amber greasy sword of light from the lamp outside narrowed to a point.

I went upstairs to see how my neighbour was. It was rare that I visited him after nightfall. There were no lights on in his flat. The mere act of walking upstairs had started my headache off again. I was encaged on my left side by quivering bars that were constantly moving towards but never occupied less than half of my field of vision. My view to the right was unobstructed. The sodium cube outside the third-floor window cast an orange unreal glare on the living-room wall, on the polished surface of the table that had not been there previously, and on the armour and weapons of the soldiers gathered round it, gambling or watching the game, some seated, some standing, all absorbed. A tableau vivant, based on some picture by Georges de la Tour, only here the light was not flickering soft candlelight or rich red firelight but the orange of the sodium, the light that gives modern nightbirds their pallor. The soldiers wore mid-seventeenth-century uniforms — 'casaques', buff coats or breastplates and a sort of helmet that was neither a typical morion nor a Dutch pot though related to both. They were all young and beardless, armed with swords. Among the seated card-players was a masked woman with a kissing patch on her lip, a square-cut bodice and an open ruff, who wore, perched roguishly on top of corkscrew curls, an incongruous but stylish military cap. She kept stretching her neck, tilting her head as if in laughter although no sound issued from her jaundice-barred throat. Two of the soldiers who were standing had features as delicate as any girl's, but their looks were somewhat spoilt by the sickly amber light. Their lips moved as if in speech but soundlessly.

CHAPTER FOUR

The following morning, I went upstairs at the usual time to find my neighbour still asleep on the couch. His snores were imperious, seignorial. While he slept I lifted the duster that covered his manuscript. The sheet on top was covered with minute handwriting. I had to stoop to read it. The underlined heading read *Secret Memoranda concerning my enemies.* The snores had ceased without my being aware of it. My neighbour was watching me. I started, cringed even, at the unusual intensity of his stare. He seemed untroubled by my spying.

'Read it!' he commanded. 'It concerns you.'

The subject of the first memorandum was d'Artagnan:

D'Artagnan's physiognomy, his outward character, is substantially the same as the Tarot Cavalier d'Epées — his arm of iron, falcon eyes, audacity, insouciance, headlong rush into the unknown without fear or outward forethought. In actual fact, far from lacking forethought he nicely calculates when it is politic to display for the benefit of others his apparently reckless bravado in the commission of a desperate enterprise. His traits include a shrewdness often difficult to perceive. On occasion he has a talent for manipulating (blackmailing) his masters. He is the King's man through and through, professional, blunt, zealous, a reliable instrument of the royal will, but he is also waspish to his inferiors, thrasonical, a brutal casuist, an unprincipled womanizer, venal, self-justifying and hypocritical. (It is said he received the captaincy of the Grey Musketeers only because of his cunning in making Cardinal Mazarin expect a large bribe.) He has spent his life embroiled in complicated amorous-financial-political intrigues undertaken solely to further his personal ambitions. Born lucky, the pistols aimed at him (more often by wronged husbands than by the King's enemies) inevitably misfire or the ball lodges in the rafters or buries itself in the wall. A cynical closet-cavalier, he believes an affectation of virtue is the most seductive trait in a woman. Note that the Baroness, his wife, prefers a convent to life with her much-sought-after husband. The episode with Miladi is too sordid to describe. Even the legendary swordmanship of his youth was largely a question of agility in avoiding his opponent's thrusts, such agility being commonplace among the Gascons and Basques whence he derives. His appearance in middle-age: bandy-legged and squabbish. A growing paunch. A swarthy complexion. In an age of courtliness a relic of the brutal anarchic forties.

'You do not recognize yourself, Monsieur,' inquired the prisoner politely when I raised my head.

'It does not refer to me, Prince,' I said. 'But most of what you write here is a grotesque libel on a gallant and unselfish gentleman who gave his life increasing your brother's *gloire* at Maestricht in '73.'

I put as much conviction as I could into these words which came unbidden to my lips as though I had spent all morning rehearsing them.

'I apologize,' my neighbour said, obviously making an effort to focus on me. Through years spent behind walls he was tallow-faced, with purplish rings beneath the cavities of deeply sunk eyes. Sometimes he did indeed seem to be wearing a mask — his skin the texture of yellow parchment.

He changed the subject.

'I would be obliged, Saint-Mars,' he said with a nasal drawl, 'if you would speak with the anspessade about the excessive noise at night. The swearing, the rattle of the dice and in particular the excited shouts of the camp-followers keep me awake.'

I bowed low, promising nothing. There was no chance that I (or anyone else) could influence the youths and screaming girls who disturbed the rest of the occupants of Ruskin House. In the past every stratagem, from a civilized remonstrance (an appeal, that is, to humanity, to social justice, to remember the sick, the old, babies) to the filthiest of curses, the wildest of threats or a phone call to the police, had always proved useless.

'The miauling of cats I can stand, Saint-Mars,' he said as I was leaving. 'And even the rattle of the tric-trac pegs.'

I discovered a little later that he had drawn tram-lines, as though crossing a cheque, across the character sketch of d'Artagnan. The word MORT in large detached capitals filled the space between the rails.

Some six months after the arrival of the recluse the pattern of our relationship was suddenly and drastically changed. I woke one morning to the sound of the door bell being rung continually upstairs. I dressed hurriedly just in time to answer the ringing at my own door. A sallow, toad-faced little woman with bulging cheeks and a long neck, a large mole just below the right eye, introduced herself to me as Miss Rampick, the sister of my neighbour upstairs. Did I know if he was in? She had been ringing the bell for ten minutes. Mephitic blasts rose from the ground floor as we ascended the steps together. The dust and ashes blown out of the rubbish chutes made my eyes water and started me coughing so that I had to wait a few moments before I was sufficiently in command of myself to insert the key in the lock.

Once I had unlocked the door she made it plain she didn't want me to stay. She almost slammed the door in my face. But she spent less time upstairs than I imagined she would. I had just finished my coffee when she was back, tapping imperiously on the glazed square in the door and walking straight in when I opened the door so that I had to press myself back against the wall to let her pass.

I didn't take in her first words, intimidated by her natural air of authority and by the sibilance, the incisive 'attack' of such a weak, small voice that always seemed to be fighting to master inaudibility. Mistakenly I thought I recognized the paper crumpled in her hand as the pictures sellotaped to my neighbour's wall. When she realized I was staring at the ball of paper rather than attending to her, she tossed it, without a word, into the fire.

Miss Rampick was not a woman who wasted words. Her brother was in no condition to look after himself; that was the substance of what she told me. He would have to be removed to the family home immediately. Unfortunately he had made it plain to her that he would go only if accompanied by his 'gaoler'. (She pronounced the word deliberately though she winced as she said it.) She would recompense me of course for the expense incurred. 'Please' and 'Thank you' did not feature in her vocabulary that day. She made a wry face when she noticed a Dumas novel on my camp-bed. Her voice (she was perhaps fifty) had a steely ring to it even though it was so feeble and monotonous.

Before she left she took a writing-pad from her handbag and wrote her address (in a town about forty miles away). She didn't ask if I knew the town but without more ado made a very creditable sketch of the most direct route from the station to her house, replacing her fountain-pen in her handbag and getting to her feet in one movement as soon as she had marked our destination, *No. 1 Blackhorse Terrace*, with a cross.

When she had gone I half-expected there would be a complete transformation in my neighbour but Marchiali/ Rampick was seated as usual at his card-table, writing furiously.

'I fully understand the arrangements you have made with La Voisin,' he said when he heard me enter. 'You have my word that I will not try to esape. Forgive me now if I don't say more today.'

And he was writing again as rapidly as though there had been no interruption. I made a low leg in the doorway to his un-heeding back.

It was to be several days before I played my part as gaoler and escort.

I received a letter from Miss Sylvia Rampick asking me to wait for National Carriers to collect the trunk which it seems she must have packed while she was with her brother. On the first day after the trunk was collected we were to set forth. I was welcome to the few sticks of furniture in her brother's rooms. Strangely enough, as far as I could tell, he didn't mind leaving his couch and the card-table — two items of furniture I expected him to be particularly attached to. The thought of the journey loomed over me, blackened the horizon. For someone like me it was a major expedition.

In fact our walk through rainy streets to the station was tense but uneventful as was the wait for the train on a more or less empty platform. A funereal goods train (leaden cylinders as long as passenger coaches) passed through the station. Then, for a short while, a Scottish express was drawn up directly in front of us. Rain cascaded in two places from the decorative wooden pendants of the awning valance on to the shiny black carriage roofs. My companion seemed oblivious both of the sight of the train and the crash and clatter of the cascading water. Usually when I glanced at him his eyes were shut. And he neither started nor opened his eyes at the abrupt, bellicose loudspeaker voice. A porter scrutinized me. His gaze rested even longer on my companion who was reasonably dressed in a long overcoat but looked like a blind stripling who had suddenly aged.

I kept looking out for the yellow-fronted metameres that shuttle to and fro between local towns and at last made them out, a series of four turning towards the station on a wide curve.

There was no through train even though the distance involved is under forty miles. It was colder and squallier at the next station. The strong wind sent twisted newspapers and other detritus bounding along over the oil-blackened sleepers in the gulf between platforms. The glass-and-iron roof was reflected in several puddles on the platform. At this station the people waiting were either old, apparently incurious as regards other travellers, or, if that were possible, were themselves odder-looking than the Man in the Iron Mask. Besides a couple of spruce, trilby-hatted sexagenarians with carrier bags who examined each of the posters and notice-boards, there was a shivering Indian woman in a sari, a short, dumpy, apple-cheeked woman with a basket, and a youth with thick goggles and an even longer coat than my companion's who ran stumblingly along the platform for no apparent reason, his open coat flapping, to stand unnaturally still where the platform is no longer covered, braving the onslaught of wind and rain. Several dwarfish bandy-legged ancient porters, custodians of that vast, high, draughty (and now almost forsaken) Temple of Steam, emerged from doorways on the far platform and disappeared into others.

Rampick seemed disturbed by the incessant ringing of a telephone. The ringing came from somewhere behind a row of high, boarded windows and yellow-tinted fanlights. Rampick opened his eyes and looked round several times. The ringing continued until the train arrived.

On the first train he had repeated: 'You have my word I will not try to escape', accompanied by a beseeching smile that I interpreted as meaning that he hoped we were, in fact, escaping together to the frontier, to Belle-Isle, wherever his hopes were just then tending. (When he spoke my heart thudded and I looked round but there was no one to overhear.) On the second train he said loudly and distinctly, with a rather crazy smile: 'And they set out for Boulogne, where towards evening they arrived, their horses covered with foam and sweat.' He declaimed this so loudly that the driver turned to look at us but he couldn't have heard what was said as the sliding door between the cab and our empty non-smoking compartment was fortunately closed just then. Only later did it slide open and I was on tenterhooks that Rampick would declaim something else. I offered him mints. He refused them with a commanding look.

The wind howled, it battered the windows of the diesel coach; the train rocked on the curves, and no doubt to Rampick it was the impatient horses that made the post-chaise shake and jounce, for, in a thrilling whisper, when we were practically at our destination, he expressed the hope that the postilions, as on a former famous occasion, were deaf and dumb. He covered his face with his hands as the train slowed entering the station. For a moment I thought he had recognized the place until I noticed a workman in a hooded black and orange jacket, a sledge-hammer at his feet, standing next to the ruins of the former station building. To Rampick the man's attitude and the sledge-hammer (perhaps even the wasp-like brilliance of his clothing) must have seemed sinister and I had difficulty getting him to walk past the workman, who in fact seemed to stare at us both with malevolent curiosity.

CHAPTER FIVE

*He was a sort of madman whom they had
been obliged to shut up in the Bastille for
his follies, without any hope of his ever
getting out. He indeed died there . . .*

Memoirs of d'Artagnan   COURTILZ DE SANDRAS

In spite of Miss Rampick's lucid directions I took the wrong turning. Almost immediately we came to a large sand-blasted church along one side of which there was a large trefoil window, the hub at the centre of a wheel of smaller cinquefoil windows. A little further on Rampick stopped by some black-and-gilt lacquered railings, attracted by the fleur-de-lis terminals. He resisted my pressure on his arm to move on, like a wilful dog straining against the leash. By contrast, he completely ignored the nineteenth-century streets, the parallel rows of two-up and two-down cottages just behind the station, and such signs of the twentieth century as the occasional parked car or the half-open fan of a gasoline rainbow in a long steep street that was macadamed for the first section but still had the original setts higher up.

Facing the blank end-walls of those parallel stone streets, the superior houses of Blackhorse Terrace had small gardens, massive bay windows, and numerous steps to the front doors. The end house was Miss Rampick's, its paintwork dirty and flaking, neglected like a haunted house in a film. The garden was a small-scale wilderness, with two huge lorry tyres sprouting weeds and a greenish lozenge-shaped stone like a headstone leaning back against the rough bark of a small tree.

The haunted house had an attic. The room the Man in the Iron Mask would shortly occupy? When Miss Rampick came to the door it struck me why she hadn't met us at the station. She was ashamed to be seen out of doors in company with her strange-looking brother. She hardly glanced at the wretched man, and made no attempt to greet him, concentrating all her attention on his keeper.

Basing my conjecture on her previous behaviour, I thought her chief worry would be how to get rid of me quickly and at the same time not appear monstrously ungrateful and inhospitable. In fact I was totally mistaken. In her own home that day she was only too anxious to bring up the subject of remuneration, of her great indebtedness to me. She wanted me to promise to visit her unfortunate brother as often as I could. She even hinted that what she needed was a suitable male lodger. I must have noticed the deplorable condition of the outside of the house. It was unavoidable just at present. She had a demanding full-time job and no man to help her.

I was surprised by the contrast between the dilapidation outside and the immaculate appearance of the rooms within. I was not prepared, either, for her dog, a sulphurous, foisty spaniel of advanced age. The dog was always at my ankles while I was standing and lay down between my calves and the easychair when I sat down. The woman obviously doted on the smelly animal. The dog, like his mistress, ignored Rampick.

While Miss Rampick was talking to me, her brother, seated in a winged armchair by the window, gazed sadly down at the corner of the fender. Suddenly the phone rang. With no hesitation he moved quickly to it, grabbed the receiver by the mouthpiece like a club and crashed the earpiece ferociously down on the window-sill. The ringing stopped. Satisfied he calmly replaced the receiver on its cradle.

Miss Rampick had her eyes shut and seemed to be swaying. The spaniel did its best to trip me but I got to the window and took Rampick by the arm, steering him across the room to the door. At the foot of the stairs he paused and looked upwards. I was just behind him. I heard him whisper, still looking upwards: 'Is this the secret staircase to the Queen's Oratory?'

'I am afraid not, your Highness,' I told him. 'But take courage. It is simply the staircase that leads to your new quarters.'

He started at my voice, then sighed loudly, rather a theatrical sigh, and began to climb the stairs.

The attic was prepared for him: a camp-bed under the sloping roof, a stool, a card-table folded in the corner, his portmanteau in another corner. I set down my 'adidas' bag containing his clothes. Rampick perched on the edge of the bed, still wearing his long overcoat.

'I recognize my old cell, Besmaux,' he said with a melancholy smile. 'My old quarters. I have come full circle.'

I helped him out of his clothes into the bed. He closed his eyes as soon as he lay down. Exhausted by the unusual activity of the day he seemed to fall asleep at once.

When I returned to the living-room the toad-faced Miss Rampick said: 'He won't hear the phone up there.' I interpreted this as signifying he would be a prisoner henceforward in the attic but Miss Rampick went on to say that before long she was sure it would be necessary to commit him to an institution. Doctors had told her that his delusion had become so deeply rooted in every aspect of his real and imaginary existence that it was unlikely it could ever be got rid of without killing him. And in her own mind she was sure this was so. That afternoon I learned from Miss Rampick something of the background of my neighbour's mania. I stayed in her living-room perhaps two hours while she related his life story in a factual, detached kind of way.

'I can tell that you feel a genuine affection for Philip and have only tried to help him by humouring his fancies,' she said, adding that she believed any such attempt to humour him by playing charades was mistaken. (Although no worse than the psychiatrist's useless therapy.)

She seemed most interested in finding out if I had any information to give her about his arrival at the flats. In his flight from her care he had been aided and abetted by a misguided friend (more culpable, less disinterested than myself) who believed herself to be the reincarnation of Prince Rupert. In other respects she was infinitely more practical and worldly than her poor brother.

I told Miss Rampick that I hadn't myself observed her brother's arrival at the flats but that later before I became involved at all with him I had been given a description by a garrulous old woman who lives on the same landing. According to this woman Rampick had arrived in a small van and had

taken no part in carrying the few sticks of furniture and a bed
settee upstairs. The poor young man (the old woman described
all but the most decrepit of men as 'young') seemed to be some
kind of invalid. There had been another man, she told me. (She
had nothing to say about him.) And there had been a strapping
young woman.

I recalled that when I had first seen Rampick's companion
she wore a long purple highwayman's cloak. She was walking
briskly, with an air of determination that could not have been
more marked had she been about to mount her horse and ride
hell for leather with a message from beleaguered Casale. (I
spared Miss Rampick this flight of fancy. The influence of
Rampick I may never shake off.)

You may have noticed that I am not reporting our two-hour
conversation directly. I have a poor memory for conversations,
an avowal that perhaps the reader may accept more readily
than acquaintances who react with scepticism (so convenient
they think it must be to have a faulty memory), believing me to
be constitutionally devious, a person with a great deal to hide.

I saw Rampick's companion from time to time on the stairs,
and at first believed her to be the sole new occupant of the
upstairs flat. I only discovered otherwise from my informant
after she had gone. At no later date did Rampick mention his
companion's existence. (Unless, conceivably, in some obscure
allusion, that meant nothing to me, he had intended to speak to
me of her.)

Her disappearance occurred perhaps a week, perhaps a
fortnight, after their arrival. The little that Miss Rampick cared
to tell me of her seemed to square with the image I had of her.
Miss Rampick's eyes told me I was being naive when I
expressed (mainly polite) surprise that the woman had stayed
with her brother such a short time. I had to admit that I had not
seen the woman's departure either.

It is rather surprising but not astonishing that I did not see
their arrival and her departure. It is not at all surprising that I
did not hear my recluse neighbour upstairs. In retrospect, it is
rather odd that I did not hear the woman's voice or movements
during the days she was living above me.

I expected my description of the first meeting with Rampick to interest the sister. My introduction to the madman (which I omitted to mention in the proper place) occurred a day or two after my conversation with the old woman. I heard sounds of weeping from above. As I had recently been told that there was an invalid upstairs the persistence of the sounds eventually shamed me into action.

I gave Miss Rampick a slightly censored version of the following:

After knocking hesitantly at his door, I lifted the letter flap and saw my neighbour stretched out on the floor of the entrance hall in a grotesque position, his face distorted with weeping. Because I had been told he was an invalid, and I thought this was some kind of attack he was having, I banged loudly on the door. At last he got to his feet, and let me in (the only time that this happened). In the circumstances he greeted me with astonishing calmness. There was a gorget of stubble under his jaw. He seemed unconscious of the strings of snot that extended across both of his wet cheeks. Of his conversation (at that time meaningless to me although so deliberately uttered) I remember: 'Excuse the tears of the Iron Mask.'

I never discovered the precise role the woman had filled for him in his history, or indeed whether he had regarded her as a woman at all. In fact, with her principal-boy face and figure, her large histrionic assertive movements and the swashbuckler's voluminous cloak, it is quite possible that she had featured in his fictions as a man, but in retrospect it seems unlikely that his tears that afternoon were totally unconnected with her desertion of him.

According to Miss Rampick her brother had never had any dealings with women.

'The whole episode of their nocturnal flight, their "elopement" was ridiculous. Philip was repelled by women. For obvious reasons.'

I didn't pursue what she meant by 'obvious reasons'. Perhaps, like me, she was in the habit of thinking in his terms. In that case the origins of his revulsion would lie in the unnatural cruelty of Anne of Austria.

When Miss Rampick said 'She must soon have learned her mistake', I took this to mean that the woman had been hoping for more intimate relations with Rampick, as well as ministering to his historical fantasies: she may have imagined that he had, like her, broad acres of worldly awareness conjoined with a fantastic belief. Or perhaps Miss Rampick simply meant the foolish woman had sought to cure him and had soon learned that this was impossible.

Generally Miss Rampick's undisguised hostility towards the woman created more heat than light when she spoke of her. One fact I knew about her: it was not much of a conversational gambit but I remarked on it nevertheless. I had noticed that she had an unusually deep voice. She had said 'Good morning' to me huskily on the second occasion that we passed on the dusty stairs. Seeing her close up I remember thinking that her handsome florid features were seen to better advantage from a distance. (Even her splendid chestnut hair seemed coarse close to.) Larger than life, she was comparable to a statuesque opera singer, colossal at close quarters, impressive from beyond the footlights. The contrast between her animated, large high-coloured face and Rampick's waxen half-face must have been as great as that between Brenda's younger, comelier broad-cheeked good looks and my own exanimate features.

It has taken until now for me to recall that Brenda used to refer to me as 'Mask-face'. Especially when I had too much to drink. And unfortunately I was only too conscious of the justice of her words when I stared back at that creamy mask in the bathroom mirror. In fact I have more of a mask-like countenance than Rampick. His face, though narrow, had certain attractive irregularities.

To finish, however, with Rampick's companion, because, after all, I never knew her and never learned more about her from Miss Rampick. It is strange that I don't know her name, that Miss Rampick, who surely must have known it, never referred to her by name. My own scruples in not asking point-blank may seem incredible to some. They were typical of me.

I was not anxious to prolong my stay although the thought of the return journey did not appeal to me either. My eventual leave-taking was abrupt and embarrassed. I did not look back at Miss Rampick in her doorway. I did not glance up to the attic window where, conceivably, the madman was already posted.

Almost immediately, so it seemed, I was back at the station where only the booking-hall and the footbridge remained intact among the cordoned-off ruins. Although it may sound far-fetched, I was even more fearful of the return journey alone than of the apparently more demanding outward journey as Rampick's escort. Maybe it was simply that I could not persuade my scattered thoughts that the worst part of the ordeal was over. Just as Rampick was condemned to have an imagination only for imprisonment, it seems I only have a lively imagination for disasters (which rarely happen). In this case, despite an excess of caution and a chronic indecisiveness (the abyss between the platform edge and the high step of the railcar seemed to invite me to plunge down beneath the wheels), I arrived back safely to find Brenda waiting for me at the door of my flat.

She had come to complain about the madman upstairs who had frightened her to death 'making faces at the window'.

My nerves still in splinters I pushed past her un-ceremoniously and tried, unsuccessfully, to shut the door in her face.

I walked from room to room, forcing her to follow me, both of us growing angrier every second.

Then, in a flash of inspiration, as she mentioned the amount it had cost to have her coat cleaned, I told her she could have his furniture in compensation.

'He has gone,' I told her. 'He doesn't want it. He gave the lot to me.'

I lent her the key to the flat which I was supposed to have already handed over to the Rent Office at the Town Hall.

Around midnight I heard sounds of furniture being moved above my head. Later the key was dropped through the letter-box.

A rickety chair and the fablon-covered card-table (ink-stained and ripped) were the only two items she didn't take.

CHAPTER SIX

I am the brother of the King of France — a
prisoner today — a madman tomorrow.
French gentlemen and Christians pray to
God for the soul and the reason of the son of
your masters. (The message inscribed on
the silver plate. The Vicomte de Bragelonne
— Dumas)

One evening a local paper was pushed through my letter-box by mistake. I began reading a paragraph dealing with an airgun attack on a local train. A window had been shattered. Passengers (a woman, a small child) had needed treatment for cuts. I was thinking vaguely that had he been a passenger on that train Rampick would have naturally assumed he was being fired at by assassins. (I was so used to entering into the spirit of the thing that I imagined scarlet tunics in a spinney overlooking a railway cutting, a glint of muskets resting on crocs thrust down among the bracken.) Then I noticed the name Rampick (misspelt Rempick) in a tiny paragraph which stated that Philip Edgar Rempick, 47, of Blackhorse Terrace was recovering in Barkworth Royal Infirmary from injuries sustained in a recent fall.

During the same week I received a letter from Rampick's sister describing the accident. Rampick had climbed out through the attic window and had fallen or thrown himself down on to the flags in the backyard. At first he had not been expected to live. He had been wearing his 'fancy dress' — the frilly shirt, the extra long woman's wig and the mask. Miss Rampick had removed the mask (the wig had fallen off) before the ambulance-men arrived.

She repeated, perhaps word for word, what she had told me some weeks earlier: that she knew I felt a genuine affection for her unfortunate brother and had tried to help by humouring him in his fancies. This was why she was forwarding some of the more lucid of his recent writings to me as a memento. The bulk of his endless scribblings she had already destroyed in his absence.

An account of the suffering her brother's condition had caused her over so many years (and in spite of the burden he had become, I must understand that she had stood out against shock treatment and personality-altering drugs) filled the remainder of her letter which surprisingly contained no direct reproaches for my not having been to see them.

The following pages are a fair copy of those given to me by Miss Rampick. Except for the odd word here and there, the handwriting is quite legible. Basically a very small hand, it has relatively large, spiky ascenders and descenders.

These pages are the only specimen of his 'diary' that I have in my possession*. A mixture of fantasy and rewriting of his historical sources and an elevated treatment, suitably modified, of recent events. His commonplace modern, local, sources I can easily recognize.

* A specimen of some other writing of Rampick's I will quote at a later stage.

'Sometimes I miss my old cell at Sainte-Marguerite. In particular I miss the sea birds. A herring-gull used to come to my cell window. [This may well be true. Author's Note] Birds used to assemble on the ramparts of the great bastion. [The mill. Author's Note] But I can imagine worse places than this. I know of a certain garret overlooking the Arsenal where prisoners are tortured in the presence of the lieutenant-criminel. A room overlooking the gallows in the Place de Grève would be worse. Infinitely worse. Pignerol and Exiles were worse.

'But I must not complain. I am reasonably comfortable here. And in this cell I am not as affected by the noise of the sentries in their guardroom as at Sainte-Marguerite's. Either there are fewer guards or their room is situated at a greater distance from my cell or the guards are all mutes like d'Herblay's postilions and play endless games of mumchance. I only see the vile witch Randon who brings me my food and empties the close stool. She says nothing (or nothing to the point) in that voice of hers — tuned to hostility.

'I cannot understand why so many dogs are kept in the Bastille. Some mornings I am woken by the brazen throats of a hundred bandogs. The whole of belling dogdom is kennelled somewhere very close yet when I look out I see nothing. Neither man nor beast. Only the same empty dusty courtyard and the same blank walls undarkened by humps or arabesques where dogs have p-ss-d which was a common sight even in fortresses where it was rare to hear a barking dog.

'Sometimes when I wake in the night I imagine a threatening figure stands by my bed. Because of his threatening attitude I call him "Signor Increpatio". It is possible he is my executioner. After a while he steals away. The cell door is closed soundlessly.

'Through being a prisoner for so long I am overwhelmed by guilt. With each breath I inhale, I inhale guilt into my lungs. I am guilty because I am I — the ACCURSED. Because of my blood, king, nobleman, or Italian prelate, whoever my father may have been, at least from my Hapsburg mother I am descended from royalty.

'Is Fouquet released yet from Pignerol? I curse him. D'Artagnan escorted him as he did me from Vaux. Like me he will die in his cage. Deservedly.

'I curse d'Artagnan because he saw in my brother the true King.

'Sometimes when I wake in the night there is a hooded figure with arms outstretched who prays silently. Then he leaves me. Sometimes a wench *stands there in the darkness — shameless in her nakedness. One of the carted community. Perhaps the Voisin girl. I smell her sunburnt flesh. I hear her deep and regular breathing. She goes softly away.*

'*I am by this time resigned to my fate (tho' it seems to me just now, as I write, at least a century has elapsed since the day I scratched a message on my plate, the day I last saw d'Artagnan and the Count de la Fère on the penal island). More than ever am I determined now to outlive my brother whose constitution must be weakened by all his youthful amours, his expensive campaigns against the Dutch, his incessant building and beautifying, and his belated piety (following a regimen unhealthily counter to his self-indulgent nature) reformed (if that is the right word) by the combination of the influence of the soiled religieuse, the Maintenon woman, and his fistula.*

'*It is best for me not to review my life — my strange distorted fairy-tale youth (deprived of mirrors and history books) under a disguised benevolent kind of house arrest, my maturity spent in one prison after another, masked or not, until I became accustomed to this life and could endure no other. For me, after that day at Vaux-Le-Vicomte, there have been no further adventures. I have had no serious illness. I do not even suffer from piles like my illustrious brother. But I have nothing positive to record either — no fêtes, no victories, no dragonnades, no Versailles, no mistresses, no illegitimate children. If my brother is the Sun King I am King of Murk-Light. My Memoirs I know are a kind of purgative for me. Without that relief I would fear for my sanity. Like Athos in his study at Castle Bragelonne I continually make additions to my Memoirs. During the night I relight my lamp and pass long hours in writing or examining my parchments. These additions to my Memoirs are my life.*

'*The worst journey of my life was the one between Pignerol and the Lérin Isles. D'Artagnan had accompanied me from Vaux to Pignerol where I was handed over to the custody of Saint-Mars. It was evident that there was no love lost between the ageing Gascon coxcomb and the modest and dignified Saint-Mars. D'Artagnan had suggested taking me himself all the way to the coast in a carriage-case. Saint-Mars, who, for such a quiet-spoken, mild-mannered man, usually succeeded in getting his own way, had decided on a sedan chair and a moderately large escort of guards and servants, and also a physician. Saint-Mars quarrelled with d'Artagnan over a plan to disguise me as a woman so that my mask would pass relatively unnoticed on the way. (At that time I showed the world a black velvet physiognomy.) Saint-Mars would not hear of a son of the House of Bourbon being degraded like that. I wore the black velvet mask until the order came from my vindictive brother that compelled the humane Saint-Mars to encase my head in iron — a helmet designed I am assured for maximum discomfort and maximum repulsiveness by Louis himself and forwarded to Sainte-Marguerite by the King's one trustworthy courier in this connexion, d'Artagnan.*

'The garrulous d'Artagnan would say to me, with the utmost seriousness, that he was solely responsible for the restoration of Charles Stuart, that he had kidnapped General Monk and arranged the future of monarchy in England, quite easily, without any fuss. To anyone sufficiently imbecile he would have claimed to have rescued Charles Stuart's martyred father and substituted Cromwell on the block. That would be hardly less outrageous than his oft-repeated claims that he had several times outwitted Mazarin and even Richelieu and had seen service with the great Cardinal at Ile de Ré in 1628 (as an infant), fought shoulder to shoulder with Toiras at the siege of Casale (as a slightly older infant) and had known the first Buckingham (in his cradle).

'That such a talkative, mendacious man should have been so trusted by Louis has never ceased to astonish me. It is said that the King enjoyed the old musketeer's coarse humour and picturesque turns of speech. The coarseness of his fanfaronades often offended Saint-Mars as on the occasion when he remarked that the one consolation of a peripatetic life was lifting the slamkin of a different hostess every night and giving a smouching kiss to each dimpled cheek and the brushwood valley between.

'A propos of the beloved son of his greatest friend, Saint-Mars told me d'Artagnan had said that Raoul de Bragelonne was so wholehearted, straightforward and idealistic about his inamorata, his simple-minded outlook was a certain recipe for disaster with La Vallière or indeed with any woman in any circumstances, but in those circumstances what woman under the sun (experienced coquette or vestal) would have resisted? What was Raoul's ingenuous devotion set against the glory, power, sensuality and proud selfishness of the King?

'A propos "The Brother" (i.e. myself) Saint-Mars reported to me that d'Artagnan had said that I might conceivably have become Louis's superior in statecraft but I could never have hoped to match his carnal

appetites. On another occasion I overheard part of a conversation between d'Artagnan and Saint-Mars: "Philippe? That dreamer on the throne?" said d'Artagnan. "He would have had no taste for kingship or the King's women."

'There was only one evening on the island of Sainte-Marguerite that I saw d'Artagnan in a relatively softened mood. It was his last night on the island and before he returned to the court he was planning to spend a few days at Lupiac. He told me rather wistfully that there were times when he wished he might be incarcerated in perpetual house-arrest in one of the corner tourelles of his ancestral home with a perpetual view of Gascony, enjoying the Gascon climate, instead of being at the King's constant beck and call, day and night, taking his rest as best he could, on hard chairs in draughty audience chambers and tapestried passages, or constantly on the move, on special missions, at staging-posts, snatching a few hours sleep between dirty sheets in dirty taverns, or three-fourths unconscious in the saddle; a man like him, a man of the smiling leisurely South, condemned to spend his days on the alert, always needing to ward off treacherous thrusts to his back (the calumny of his enemies: politicians' weapons — worse by far than cold steel!) in the gusty, rainy, smurry, rheumaticky North.

'It was the nearest I came to seeing the Chevalier in a sympathetic light. Nevertheless I was relieved the following morning when a boat took him back to the mainland. I never saw him afterwards. Saint-Mars told me that he died in '73.

'I think myself that I might have been content in my prison with a view of the sea but there must have been orders that I was to be forbidden a sea-facing cell, perhaps because of the possibility of a fisherman or look-out on a passing merchantman catching a glimpse of my iron visage at the window. When there was sunlight in my cell (which was rare because of the massive projecting tower obstructing my view) the sun and the sound of the waves, the soughing of the pines and the call of sea-birds revealed to me the azure of the unseen Mediterranean.

'Unseen from the day I arrived till the day I was transferred back here to the capital, suddenly, unaccountably, openly; my face uncovered on the public highway, travelling by a ramshackle public conveyance, like a common felon with a single gaoler, the tired, overweight, careworn Saint-Mars.

'The times are obviously so changed, I am so changed, the King's position is so invulnerable, the succession guaranteed, that no one fears my

resemblance any longer. And to show his contempt for me the King has entrusted me to the care of a bawd and witch (that I thought had been burnt years ago with the little Brinvilliers woman and a pack of sorcerers) to poison or drive me mad.

'Perhaps my iron face-guard is a curio already, rusting away in a corner of my old spacious cell on that far-off island, preserved together with my chair, my table, platter, knife, fork and silver tankard, a spectacle for the curious and idle in years to come. Since returning here I have not seen Saint-Mars once. I am afraid he is ill. I had never seen him look so unlike himself as on the journey here. All the spirit has gone out of him in recent years. An unpopular man, on account of his silences, the fits of trembling that afflicted Saint-Mars were also regarded by many as the outward sign of repressed choler. His naturally serious lofty manner (snobbishly derided in a former sergeant-major of musketeers) was mistaken, especially by the Protestants imprisoned with me in Richelieu's maritime citadel, for coldness and unkindness. But no man, I am sure, could have had a higher conception of duty and honour than Saint-Mars. His unswerving devotion to his royal master I found no less admirable than his attention to my welfare in captivity.

'It is inconceivable that Saint-Mars ever questioned the justice of my being kept in perpetual imprisonment (he is the sort of man who was born to follow orders without question) yet given the constraints imposed on him by the King and Louvois, he has done everything possible to alleviate the misery of my condition, obtaining books for me, good food and wine, the latest fashionable clothes, and indulged me in my weakness for lace and linen of a quality that might have satisfied the Queen, my fastidious mother.

'Over the years his manner to me has been unfailingly courteous and respectful. From the early days when I was lodged in the lower tower at Pignerol, during those long years spent on a rock in the Sea of Provence, Saint-Mars has never altered one whit in his manner to me, he has never presumed on our long acquaintance to become in the slightest degree familiar.

'Before I learned that he had requested to be transferred to the capital, it had not occurred to me to suspect that life was very tedious for Saint-Mars on the Island. He did not seem a man who yearned for company. Perhaps the good man was homesick for northern landscapes, for his château at Palteau?

'He was a large man and I know he suffered acutely from the heat. Most days in summer he told me that he used to walk by the sea-shore for coolness (for the flying spray to damp his brow) or stroll in the pine woods. Mopping his brow with the handkerchief that was often in his hand, he liked to watch me writing. I wrote with enthusiasm because it was an occupation that had been forbidden me in earlier years. Happy to see his prisoner so engrossed, Saint-Mars would flatter me that it was not impossible I was engaged on something of permanent value, like the works of M. Racine, that would outlast the meretricious buildings of my brother. (It was a paradox of Saint-Mars's character that he seemed to dislike Louis the man as absolutely as he revered the monarch.)

'When I was not in the mood for reading or writing, we would play bassett or tables, billiards or chess. Saint-Mars had little small talk. Little in the way of incident befell him on the island. He would apologize for retelling old anecdotes d'Artagnan had told him years before. (In retrospect, years after d'Artagnan's death, Saint-Mars seemed to have grown almost fond of the braggart Gascon.)

'During one of our conversations I remember telling Saint-Mars that, compared to the pikeman's manly breastplate and morion, the uniform of the musketeers was unfortunately reminiscent of King Henri III and his mignons, by which I meant, partly, the effeminate briefness of the sky-blue cloak-and-tunic (that nowhere near reaches the tops of the thigh-length riding boots) and, even more, the silver-embroidered crucifix insignia and the ecclesiastical delicacy of the clouds of snow-white cambric falling to the shoulders. In saying this I admit I was chiefly motivated by spite although, I think, a reasonable case can be made out for this view. Immediately, by the pained expression on Saint-Mars' face and his resolute but transparent attempts to hide his displeasure by mopping his brow with his hand-kerchief, I was made aware that something remained of a long-cherished ambition to have been himself Captain-Lieutenant of Musketeers. We sat in silence for the rest of the evening. When the Protestant weavers (the Scribbler and the rest) began their psalm-singing, Saint-Mars made this an excuse to leave and sent de Formanoir to keep me company. (De Formanoir was a harmless man I could never abide who would pretend he believed my name was Dauger when he didn't forget himself and address me as 'Monseigneur'.)

'Perhaps, over the years, Saint-Mars simply grew tired of my company. To be confronted daily across the gaming-board by eyes set deep within the *occularium of a great visor, to attempt to be normal, even affable, with such a freakish companion, must have been an intolerable burden for the worthy man to have sustained for decades. And I was often silent. I grew unused to company. I was embarrassed that my voice behind the "bellows" visor seemed to borrow its timbre from the iron.*

'Whenever I happened to touch, by accident, the moveable chin-piece of my helmet and then looked down to see the fine lace at my wrists and my delicate well-manicured hands, the contrast made me feel myself to be half man, half ferruginous monster. My only comfort was, that as I always ate alone, there was no one to observe the inevitably grotesque propalinal movement of my chin-piece as I chewed my food.

'In the end I convinced myself that poor Saint-Mars could not bring himself to look at my iron mask and thought himself the unhappiest of men to have so little respite from my company (the King, while paying the gaoler a handsome salary for the inconvenience, refused to grant Saint-Mars permission to absent himself for an extended period from his command).

'After years feigning to be inured to captivity (Saint-Mars' "ancient" tranquil prisoner) there came a day when I felt unable to endure the pretence any longer. I lifted the close helm from my shoulders and placed it in a corner. Then I waited to be granted a quick death for my disobedience. It was evening when Saint-Mars knocked and entered my cell. He bowed to the high-backed chair where I would normally have been sitting. He made a remark about sending for candles. (The day had been overcast and showery — it was perhaps later than the time Saint-Mars normally came to sit with me.) And then he stiffened on perceiving me in the darkest corner, a timid rebel, bareheaded, unmasked. His hand grasped the hilt of his old-fashioned verdun. He glanced round as if to make certain we were alone. No exclamation, no imprecation, as I recall, escaped his lips. He remained in this pose for several seconds before turning on his heel. Although I knew nothing of this at the time (I believed he had gone to fetch Ru or de Formanoir), it later transpired that Saint-Mars had communicated to the King an urgent request to free me from the condition relating to the wearing of the iron mask in private because of a chronic skin complaint (scalp fungus) and general ill-health associated with constriction and chafing. Contrary to Saint-Mars's expectations, my brother promptly granted this extraordinary dispensation. (And nowadays, of course, no one seems to care whether I wear a mask or not. This incredible

46

change in attitude has come about almost imperceptibly and I suppose is no more remarkable than a change in political alliances or standards of morality.)

'*My interest in continuing to live had revived wonderfully during the few moments suspense when there seemed a possibility that Saint-Mars might use his sword. Although he never spoke of this afterwards I think, in his letters to the King and the Minister of War, he must also have stressed my altered appearance — my hair I know is now white and my complexion and the cast of my features no doubt reflect the long years of a walled-up life. At this moment there are probably a dozen noblemen at court who resemble my brother more closely than I do myself.*

'*They used to claim that Louis de Cavoye and his brothers were the image of the King. At Pignerol, his elder brother, the disgraced and disinherited spy and child-murderer Eustache, was imprisoned at the same time as Fouquet. If there was ever a chance of my escaping, it lay in a substitution of someone like Eustache de Cavoye for myself. But there was no chance of that without the connivance of Saint-Mars, and despite his great respect (and compassion) for me, Saint-Mars would never have countenanced any treachery to the basic injunctions of the King.*

'*I first began to suspect that my circumstances had altered for the worse on the way here at the vast relay station as grandiose as the stables of an English duke. Then again, when I was received at the Bazinières Tower, I sensed that something was amiss. My nerves were so on edge that when a string snapped on my guitar I felt compelled to pick up the offending instrument and smash the belly on the window ledge. And now to have the witch Anne Randon as a fellow prisoner and serving maid!*

'*Does the King want my life?*

'*What a question after all these years? After the countless assurances Saint-Mars has given me on that score?*

'*Old associations, dismal associations, confused me at first. I confused Saint-Mars with Besmaux. I imagined the narrow steep staircase to my cell to be Anne of Austria's private staircase in the Louvre. I mistook the witch Randon for Catherine Monvoisin. It has taken me weeks to get my thoughts in better order.*

'*The present Governor of the Bastille is my old friend Bénigne d'Auvergne de Saint-Mars though I never see him now. The King's Lieutenant is called du Jonca. I never see him. M. de Rosarges is the Major of the Bastille. I see no one. Only the witch, Randon.*

'My conclusion is that the old King has repented of his recent leniency to me or I have mortally offended Saint-Mars without realizing it. I am no longer even sure that the man who brought me here was my old friend, Bénigne. Bénigne, of course, is a big man and has become paunchy with age but could that Lag Belly who sweated opposite me on the endless journey here (drinking continually from a huge borrachio that bemused but never refreshed him) really have been the "prudent and wise Saint-Mars".

Now I think of it, how could I have confused my noble-hearted gaoler with that gross peasant whose deep navel and the folds of whose drooping belly, covered with a floss of reddish-gold hairs, were continually showing between his sweat-stained shirt and his breeches?

'My angel-bed is hard. The view from my cell is indescribably mean. As I write this, the carline has just been with some food. Her beaked profile is enough to deserve the pilliwinks or to be stabbed with a gadling. I know that mixed with the food she brings me is Stinking Hellebore to cure my rages and so, as a matter of course, I upturned the platter and emptied the cup she had brought on to the floor. I extravagantly simulate the madman whenever she is near. As she was leaving I threw a knife at her back. Although the haft of the dagger was standing out between her shoulder-blades, she glanced back at me, her yellow face expressionless, then she opened the door, apparently normally, and closed it behind her. This proves, to my satisfaction, that she is a witch.

'As I remember them the towers of the Bastille were much higher in former days whereas now the roofs of the surrounding hovels seem hardly distinct from the walls of the fortress. Yellow smoke, puthering up from a chimneypot shaped like a royal crown, is wafted this way and rises higher.

'The rain falls incessantly on the rooftops of squalid houses. Last night the swivel-eyed dirty wench came to my bedside again. She smiled down at me and called me her little blackbird. Above the swollen brown gourd of her belly, on the underside of the globe of her left breast, there is a large birthmark, the exact shape, in silhouette, of the iron mask, an armet with "bellows" visor. This hagseed (or succubus) is the girl I formerly identified with the Voisin daughter, transported years ago, after the affair of the poisoners, to Belle Isle to be forgotten or garrotted. It may indeed be she! There are livid marks on her neck. Her face is a dead-leaf colour. When the succubus turned to go I saw that the haft of the dagger I had *planted between the prominent shoulder-blades of Randon was standing out from her plump greasy sunburnt back. The girl had a strong resemblance to the homely-featured, big-breasted maid of Mme. de Montespan, that Mlle des Oeillets whom my satyr of a brother used if her mistress was engaged for a few minutes on her close-stool when the master's desire was overwhelming. (His royal puissance being such that unlike lesser mortals he needed almost no time at all "to restore exhausted nature".)*

'Towards the end of my stay on the sea-girt rock I received a visit from the Marquis de Louvois. In his honour, as though I were a tragedian on the stage, I wore the iron mask that had been gathering dust for a number of years. The Marquis was all flourish and obsequiousness but I strummed my guitar while he delivered his prepared speech, thus destroying the fluency of his discourse. I only spoke once to say that I hoped my brother, his royal master, was quite well. After a few more stammered words the Marquis presented me in silence with a court sword (a flamberge with a gilded hilt — the hilt and a stump of blade soldered to its steel scabbard); a set of handsomely carved chess pieces; and a broad-brimmed hat decorated with gold lace and ostrich plumes which I immediately clapped on to my visored helm (as a tame monkey might have done a similar gewjaw) to my visitor's extreme discomfiture. The Marquis did not say that the gifts came from the King. There was no letter addressed "To my hated sibling. . ." I still relish (in memory) the spectacle of the great Minister humbly courteous, scraping and flourishing with his hat as he withdrew silently, apparently crestfallen, to the door of my cell while I nodded my iron head and plucked extravagantly at the strings of my guitar.

'I woke this morning to the sound of hooves on the cobbles below. At times I heard a muffled drum. I hear it as I write. Also gut-scrapers and trumpeters. Inarticulate cries.

'If I die before Saint-Mars, has he orders to burn all my manuscripts? And if Saint-Mars is the first to die? What then? These few pages I can roll up tightly, conceal in the flue of the small fireplace in my cell. However my bulky "Memoirs" cannot be disposed of in that way. It is a problem I must give much thought to solving.

'Clop of hooves again. More drum taps.

[A final paragraph was scored through heavily but I managed to decipher it. Author's note]

'Half the population of this kingdom is wearing Louis Carthorse hats. For sale in Paris, Rheims, Dijon, Boulogne. 70 different kinds, the largest for the King.'

After the departure of the Man in the Iron Mask, I missed having a role to play as much as if I had been a genuine confidant deprived of his royal master. Although Rampick had overestimated the importance of the part I played in our conversations, during the time I knew him I had learned to make good use of snippets of information. I would introduce them with a certain measure of artfulness and retract them, more or less naturally, if they appeared to disturb him. Considering his very complicated system of 'personal' historical references I could not expect to approach him without sometimes making gross errors.

Once I mentioned that M. de Wardes had been arrested by order of the King, this seemed to me a reasonable thing to happen, believing de Wardes, after Dumas, to have been an unpleasant schemer. The news so disturbed Rampick, that I hastily added it was a rumour I had heard in the taverns, and coming from the particular source it had, I was doubtful myself about its accuracy. His suspicion, I recall, did not disperse immediately. He was not, however, chronically mistrustful and alert in an aggressive way as madmen are commonly reckoned to be. In that particular instance he merely gave me a stern melancholy warning against repeating idle gossip.

If Rampick had still been living in the upstairs flat I would probably have worked into our conversation the 'juggernaut' I saw one day with the legend ROCHEFORT on the side, conflating that with d'Artagnan's enemy and mentioning perhaps that I had seen someone with a remarkable resemblance to Rochefort. I had learned always to introduce some kind of qualification at this point because I could never be certain whether the date on his invisible calendar, the Undiscoverable Hour and Day locked inside his head, was in the late sixteen-sixties or in one of the decades following up to 1703 or, and this was more than likely, fluctuated according to how he was feeling.

'I have seen Rochefort' I would have told Rampick, or 'I have seen someone remarkably like Rochefort' I would have hedged, 'surrounded by armed guards on the road to Vincennes'. The ball would then have been in his court. He would have been free to make his own deductions based on my idle invention. It had become a conditioned reflex. I still expected to continue playing this game even now that there was no satisfaction to be derived from it. I visualized the container lorry and the dirty narrow street along which it was thundering. The passage of the monstrous 'juggernaut' shook the condemned houses to their foundations. That was all there was to it. And yet had Rampick still been occupying the upstairs flat, on one of his good days he could have made me forget the reality in the elaborate fiction he would have constructed around my distortion of the truth. Even if he had not been in an expansive mood, by no more than a few words he would have transformed the false information he had been given, saying something like 'It is high time *that* man were hanged in earnest'. A remark like that, from his lips, would sound so natural, so reasonable, that I would be drawn some way towards the magnet of *his* 'reality' which rejected container lorries, aircraft, television, and the like, even when directly confronted by the evidence of their existence. Entering into the spirit of the thing, I would seem to recall Rochefort, tragically altered, broken in spirit, his cloak covered with dust, surrounded by ironclad men (ironclad because the container had been of grey metal), my own wavering apathetic sense of reality crumbling before my neighbour's invincible belief.

It is ironical that it was not until after my neighbour's removal that I came across *The Memoirs of d'Artagnan* by Gatien Courtilz de Sandras in the town's Reference Library. At once I saw that this had been a major source of some of Rampick's knowledge. For example it must have coloured his view of d'Artagnan (so unlike my own Stevensonian admiration) and led him to regard the celebrated Gascon as a shrewd brutal gigolo.

Because I dislike reading at tables with students and down-

and-outs, I borrowed the three large handsome volumes without permission (just as Dumas himself more creatively stole the French version). I skipped a good deal of the more or less official history, court intrigue, royal alliances, Louis's campaigns. But I read the intimate *chroniques scandaleuses* avidly, gathering material (even making notes) as though it would improve my performance. This was absurd of course because the drama's six months' run had terminated with the removal of the chief character.

I also began to speculate obsessively about other possible sources upon which Rampick could have drawn. Other sources of inspiration. His age, I thought, made it likely that one or other of the Hollywood musketeer films influenced him in childhood or adolescence as much as the Dumas novels. Rampick would have been at a very impressionable age (under ten) at the time of the release of the silent *Iron Mask*, in his late teens or early twenties when the later James Whale version came to his local cinema.

Striking, poetic photographs from the silent Douglas Fairbanks version show a headpiece for the King's brother the forepart of which suggests the face of a gorilla (with a huge projecting muzzle of a visor) while the back exactly corresponds to the shape of the human cranium, the surface patterned or networked as though with imitation veins. These, from certain angles, give an appearance of extreme fragility to the monster who, from the neck downwards, is the antithesis of forbidding jungle beast or grim armoured warrior — the limbs and trunk belong to a nobleman somewhat disordered and negligent in his dress but nevertheless be-laced and be-satined in the pompous yet frivolous costume of the age.

One 'still' of the forlorn pitiable creature, like the fairy-tale Beast in his court finery, shows him, knife in hand, in an attitude of profound concentration, leaning forward over the table in his roomy vaulted cell, absorbed in scratching the famous 'message' on his silver platter. Once, in a dream derived from such images, I saw the prisoner exercising in a courtyard, an escort of halberdiers trailing behind his dispirited shoulders. He was deep in conversation with his gaoler, the stern but

53

considerate Saint-Mars, who, with each deferential glance, seemed to be attempting to read some expression in the unalterable iron features of the half-man by his side.

But this was the merest fragment compared to an intricate, extended dream for which the setting was the Bastille disguised as council flats, or the flats disguised as the Bastille. As the dream continued it became more and more Bastille with the occasional anachronism that disturbed me a little from time to time. Rampick believed the flats to be the citadel of the Ile Sainte Marguerite. In my dream the superstructure of a fortress with towers, assumed to be the Bastille, was added to the basic layout of Ruskin House.

The dream began in a guardroom of the Bastille, a room of exactly the same dimensions as my living-room in Ruskin House. With the omniscience of the dreamer, I knew straight away that the prisoner had just died. The sentries, crowded around the gaming-board, were complaining about the governor, Saint-Mars. From his sickbed Saint-Mars had given orders that the deceased prisoner's linen, clothes, bed and chairs were to be burned. But rather than being told of this I witnessed each stage of the operation in progress. (At the same time I remained in the guardroom with the dice-playing sentries.) The first stage was the bonfire of clothes and furniture. Next I saw the walls and ceiling being carefully scraped. Prayers, signs, and calendar marks were obliterated by a number of workmen who, immediately this was accomplished, began replastering and whitewashing the cell until their orders were countermanded by others to seal up the entrance. Meanwhile the chimney had been climbed, swept and examined *prestissimo* by a soot-blackened zany. The walls had been tapped for hidden cavities and the tiles taken up from the floor. References to the dead prisoner by the sentries were generally as sympathetic and respectful as allusions to Saint-Mars were hostile and denigrating. When a call of nature made me leave them, someone had just remarked that he had always been of the opinion that Saint-Mars was the madman, not his prisoner.

Anxious to relieve myself but not in the closet which seemed a possibility for an instant, I descended a dark turnstair. Holding out my hands to feel the walls, though I do not recollect my hands coming in contact with anything solid, I was soon at ground level, pushing open the forever-banging swing doors of Ruskin House. The unfamiliar courtyard I stepped out into was surrounded by battlemented walls and the silhouettes of huge extinguisher-topped towers. In the immediate proximity of the barbican were torches, evidence of drunken carouse, swaying (fraternal or fighting?) soldiery. I did my best to avoid star-splatters of recent vomit. I headed for the darkest corner of the yard but whenever I moved into deep shadow, murmuring figures would approach carrying lights. I almost collided with a sedan-chair containing an old man asleep, with wig awry, mouth wide open. The way forward was blocked by carts and broken-down carriages piled one on top of another as for a funeral pyre.

When I returned to the guardroom, the sentries were still discussing the saintly prisoner and 'that pig Saint-Mars'. A woman entered enveloped in a large riding-cloak of the kind known as a 'balandrine'. She was a sloe-eyed young woman with a good complexion and a sweet 'inner donjon' of a face surrounded by substantial 'outer baileys' of fat. She was tall, very stout, with masculine shoulders, a man's gait. Without removing her hooded cloak, the woman sat down at the gaming-table with the sentries. The woman in the half mask with the beauty spot and the military style cap smiled across at her meaningly. Now that the guards were talking freely, shouting out and gesticulating with a newly-acquired licence (the iron grip of Saint-Mars lifted from their shoulders), their delicate features seemed to have coarsened and aged. I heard whispers around me that the prisoner was not dead. A false report of the Mask's death had been broadcast as part of the plan of his escape. The surgeon-major, a priest and a lieutenant were involved, along with others. Confined to his bed, perhaps at death's door, Saint-Mars would nevertheless have roused himself immediately and broken all the conspirators on the wheel had he had the least inkling that at this very moment his lifelong prisoner was at liberty, in a carriage drawn by eight horses, approaching the frontier.

The conclusion of the dream took place in a torchlit *chapelle ardente* to which the cloaked woman led me. Several women dressed as nuns were introduced in turn. One was presented to me as Mme de Brinvilliers, a relative, I assumed, of the poisoner whose ashes had been borne away by the breeze many years ago. The Countess of Soissons was presented also and a lame woman with a ravaged face, a few strands of white hair showing, who was none other than the royal mistress that the young Vicomte de Bragelonne had died for love of, now known as Sister Louise de la Miséricorde. The group of women parted to reveal a coffin. At the same time two much larger hooded figures came forward dwarfed by their own immense shadows on the wall behind them. As a cord tightened round my neck, I realized I was to be substituted for the prisoner. Perhaps the heart and the lights had to be delivered to Saint-Mars for verification or the head to be pounded to dust. I calmly murmured 'the beast is in the toils', an expression I had long before read in the *Memoirs of d'Artagnan*.

I woke bolt upright in bed. Isolated drops of thunder-rain blundered against the window like drowsy, gorged bees deceived by the transparency of glass. Lightning flickered. In the forecourt I saw the gaunt erect figure of the prisoner standing unnaturally still in torrential rain like a menhir. A watchdog was leaping silently, relentlessly, as high as his chest. It was borne upon me that previously the roof line of the buildings opposite had seemed incomplete without a massive round tower at each corner. The towers' conical turrets gleamed through the rain, which lashed the helm of the state prisoner who recklessly exposed his iron visage to the pikemen and musketeers (mustachioed, overweight, glairy-eyed, silent-screen extras of the best quality pasteboard) who had emerged from gateway and doorway, partisans at an awkward slope, swords nervously bared. The watchdog bounded away, leaving the defenceless prisoner alone, as if he were the hub of a cart-wheel of pikes and swords. The action of raising both hands

(perhaps to remove the mask) provoked an immediate onslaught. As one man the scrimers and pikemen lunged at the
prisoner's head.

CHAPTER EIGHT

I sent a get-well card to the hospital where Rampick had been admitted. I made no effort to visit him there. Neither did I reply to his sister's letter, content to wait for further news. For weeks I had been engrossed in *The Memoirs of d'Artagnan* but I acted towards the friend who had inspired all this reading with apparent indifference. I was well aware that my behaviour was callous. And yet I continued inactive, not even seriously considering the possibility of writing or phoning Miss Rampick. Then, one day, a brief letter arrived which told me that Rampick was home again, apparently cured. And by 'cured' there was no mistaking what was meant was Rampick's delusion.

On the train I kept looking out for the mansard roofs of the red brick hospital. I had forgotten that a good view of the old building is nowadays impossible because of additional wards built close to the railway tracks. It would have been appropriate if the ward Rampick had been admitted to had been in the old part. If he had been accommodated in one of those new glass boxes high above the industrial town that must have taxed his ingenuity to the uttermost in stage-managing transformation. I could very readily believe that any daydreams and manias of my own, nurtured in darkness and solitude, would be instantly obliterated by exposure to the brash corporate reality of a large hospital. But I had far greater faith in the resistance of Rampick's obsession to external influences.

The old infirmary reminds me of a picture I once saw of the *Ecole Militaire* in Paris. For all I know the building might be a brick replica of the *Hotel de Ville* or some former royal palace in France.

Much farther away, on a hillside (snow-striped that morning but more often a pale watery green) stands the forbidding hospital for long-term patients, geriatrics, the feeble-minded, terminal cases. Its distant outline suggests a fortress with numerous squat dark stone towers and an unfortress-like skittle-shaped factory chimney. I regard the building with deep aversion: the sort of place where the old are consigned to die from the confusion and distress of being uprooted.

At the high-roofed, dingy black junction I had a lengthy wait for my connexion. Hanging name-boards creaked and swayed in an icy wind. Walking up and down to keep warm, I was thinking dejectedly that there might well be much less time than I imagined between the uncomfortable but independent present and the day when I would myself be consigned in a state of helplessness to some Castle of Desolation like the hospital on the hill. For all of us there is a finite number of days to spend at liberty, with our faculties intact, surrounded in our homes by compliant vassals (familiar objects), observing superstitious rituals, shields that only comfort us so long as real dangers are remote.

When the train arrived, the remainder of the journey took less than fifteen minutes. Since I was there last the old station had disappeared completely. The rubble had been removed. A small air-raid shelter had been erected on the up-platform to serve as a new booking-office and waiting-room. In defiance of a poster on the footbridge, *The Lord will provide all our needs in abundance*, the protection of a roof and windows had latterly been denied travellers. Even the steps were now alarmingly open-tread.

I found it impossible that morning to fix my mind on Rampick. Instead my head was full of an old daydream that had grown stale twenty years before. On my way to school, through streets very like these, I used to imagine myself returning in solitary triumph, rich and world-famous, to my home-town. The risible part of the daydream lay in the image I conjured up of a middle-aged Man of Distinction dressed in a knee-length overcoat with astrakhan collar, black homburg hat, cigar in mouth, perhaps a smart ebony cane under his arm, revisiting (*de haut en bas*) the humble scenes of his youth. Further along the street, a brutish-looking man in shirt-sleeves seemed to be participating in my resurrected day dream, as he shuffled

across the flags between his front door and the kerb edge to spit
into a black mound of melting snow.

Round the next corner a dead cat, garlanded with paper
chains, lay on another heap of frozen, part slushy snow. I stood
near it for a few moments aware that I was being watched by
Miss Rampick from her parlour window. When she realized I
had seen her, she came to the front door. This time there was no
spaniel to greet me. The dog had been put to sleep 'for his
incontinence'.

In Miss Rampick's living-room I had an appalling presen-
timent of old age. It was as if someone immensely old had
lowered himself down, at the same moment that I had sat down
on the settee, endowing me with his dim vision, his muffled
sensations. As soon as Miss Rampick had disappeared into the
kitchen, I checked to see how I looked in the mirror. I looked
pale, haggard even, but not as decrepit as I felt.

As she returned with coffee and biscuits, Miss Rampick
looked up significantly at the ceiling. She thought he might be
sleeping but I could go up and see him whenever I liked.

I would get a better reception if I saw him alone. I would find
him exactly the same. He had lapsed back into his old ways.

Miss Rampick recited medical details as though quoting
someone, perhaps the male nurse who came regularly.
Concussion, severe bruising, broken ribs, a sprained ankle, a
broken wrist, had been the known extent of Rampick's injuries.
He had made a rapid, a miraculous recovery. He was an
exemplary patient as far as his physical injuries were concerned.

'Can he get up,' I asked her.

'He *can*. He doesn't much care to.'

During those first days when she had begun to hope that he
had recovered from his delusion (Miss Rampick retained a
somewhat naive faith in an instantaneous recovery), he had
been quiet but amazingly tractable.

'The expression on his face was different. And there was no
more tomfoolery in anything he said. He used my proper name
instead of those other dreadful names he'd been calling me. He
hadn't been so normal for years. . . . But as soon as he asked for

his papers, and I told him I thought he'd finished with all that nonsense, straight away he was back to being the Man in the Iron Mask again.'

She grimaced and stirred her coffee.

'He pretended to sleep for a long time. Then he had a kind of fit. He was so bad that to calm him down I told him you'd removed his papers to a safe place before the police got their hands on them. This morning he asked to see you. I was on tenterhooks until you came . . .

'He kept shouting downstairs even while the nurse was here. It was a relief when he fell asleep . . .

'And he has a new mania now. He writes notes on the backs of playing-cards. I can see I'm going to have to provide him with paper again — either that or have him committed and get him off my hands for good . . .

'I'm very tempted to do that now . . .

'Since the accident I've only worked part time . . .'

She seemed close to tears.

'It all seems much harder to bear without poor Max,' (the spaniel).

She shrugged when I asked if she believed her brother's fall was accidental.

'Probably he thought he was escaping from the Bastille,' I said. She told me the windows no longer opened. He would have to smash his way through the glass if he tried it again. In summer his room would be stifling.

During a thaw earlier in the week the guttering from the back of the house had come down into the small garden. Like the runner of a giant sled, it lay at right angles on top of the slender matchstick of a clothes-prop. A snow-drift lay beyond it, a surviving pure white, high-finned drift. Otherwise the garden looked particularly dank and desolate, with small patches of dirty snow here and there on the muddy grass. The wood of the trellis and the rickety fence, splintered, sodden and bright green, reminded me of driftwood.

'Perhaps Philip dislodged the guttering when he fell,' said Miss Rampick.

'Then the snow avalanching down brought it right off. *He*

didn't seem alarmed by the noise. All he wanted to know was what date it was. There's no point in telling *him* the year.'

She uttered these last words slowly, with considerable venom. And then, not unexpectedly, she burst into tears.

With great reluctance I attempted to comfort her, taking care not to increase the intimacy between us. I found her more sympathetic than I had done on the day she came to the flats but no more attractive. If anything she was older-looking. She was lamentably ugly and charmless, especially when in tears!

I could not bring myself to utter her Christian name. I put my arm round her awkwardly (in silence and very briefly) and left her to make herself a pot of tea while I went upstairs to see Rampick.

The narrow stairs were dark.

The attic was dark. The curtains at both small windows were drawn to.

Rampick seemed to be asleep, feigning sleep I expected. After a few moments he spoke.

'Saint-Mars,' he said. 'Complete with fashionably disordered Steenkirk cravat.'

I was out of sympathy with him after the spectacle of his sister's distress. And what he had said was such a terribly forced opening — even though it was true that the knot of my tie had slipped — the remark seemed so far below the standards he had accustomed me to in the past that I almost felt indignant with him, as though he had palmed me off with inferior goods when I had paid good money for the genuine article.

Without saying a word, I drew aside the curtains. He put up his arm to shield his eyes. I ignored this. One of his wrists was bandaged. There were bruises on his face.

From the attic the street seemed a long way below. From this vantage point I could see skid marks. They made me think the black cat might have been killed where it now lay. When I drew the curtains at the back I saw again from a dizzy height the kitchen roof that had broken Rampick's fall. Below that, one corner of the tiny square of muddy lawn was visible and also one end of the giant sled runner. A box-tree grew between the ashpit doors and backyard gate.

'Have you brought my papers.'

A low voice behind me. (Tone almost of supplication.)

A bandaged arm raised, imploring.

I said quietly that there was no need at all for him to be anxious. His papers were locked in the desk in my office together with official dispatches from the King.

'I will keep the papers under lock and key until such time as it is safe to make them public. If that is what you wish.'

He seemed vastly relieved to hear this.

'While I was at the *Charité*,' he told me, 'there was an old decayed nobleman who had been cheated out of his birthright by his relative by marriage, the victor of Steenkirk.'

'It is the same everywhere,' he added. 'The great and glorious oppress the weak and unfortunate.'

'M. de Luxembourg himself spent several years in the Bastille before his resurgence,' I contributed boldly, not happy with 'resurgence' but pleased to have the necessary information to sustain a conversation and at the same time to give it an optimistic turn.

I had shot my bolt, however. The rest of my visit consisted of a stilted monologue by Rampick to which I could contribute nothing. After each pause, when he had finished speaking, he looked to me for some comment, some reaction, my approbation or dissent. But from necessity I was forced to remain dumb. A hesitant smile when a smile seemed appropriate was the extent of my participation.

Irritation presently showed in his eyes. For the first time I thought I saw a family likeness between Rampick and his sister.

'I am tired, Monseigneur,' I said, lamely, in extenuation of my embarrassed silence.

'You rode here from Versailles?' he inquired, suspiciously. 'You have spoken with the King?'

I pretended to be vexed in my turn. I said that I believed the King was at Marly. 'As for myself I have been busy on my estates,' I told him.

'The King has no new instructions concerning me?'

'I think the King has lost interest in both of us,' I dared to reply.

'If all the rightful heirs were to die before the King and myself, he would enthrone one of the Princes of the Blood,' Rampick murmured to himself. 'Louis, gift of God! Philippe, mongrel-lump!'

By this time I was finding it difficult to restrain my eagerness to take an immediate leave of him.

I am no lover of the twentieth century but this was ridiculous play-acting, a closet drama so precious and pointless, demanding on my part improvisation and knowledge (not to mention an appearance of sincerity and mastery of a periphrastic style) that were beyond my capabilities, and on his part a degree of self-blinding as monstrous as physical self-mutilation.

At his behest I closed the curtains. I went downstairs with the intention of leaving immediately. As I entered the living-room I could see, in the late afternoon twilight, that the table was already set for two.

I waited too long to make an excuse. No excuse presented itself to me.

'It must be a terrible strain for you,' I said to Miss Rampick. 'I am out of practice at humouring him.'

I omitted to mention the homework I had so assiduously done that had proved insufficient preparation for the actual test.

The presence of Rampick upstairs overshadowed the meal. From time to time we heard him coughing. It was the cough of a perfectly normal man.

Miss Rampick commented that she had never known him to have been troubled with a cough before his accident. Was it the sort of thing she should mention to the nurse?

I was still thinking how strange it was that there should be nothing histrionic in the sound. It was nothing like the ostentatious cough of my estranged wife when she thought she was alone. I used to interpret her cough either as a straight-forward attempt to attract my attention or an attempt to reassure herself that she was more than a vague amorphous consciousness, her vivid presence obliterated as soon as she was deprived of company.

I told Miss Rampick that Brenda had a persistent cough, and that I believed it was as much a habit as anything. 'As for your brother,' I said, 'it's probably nothing to worry about but it won't do any harm to mention it to the nurse.'

I had referred to my wife very rarely to Miss Rampick. Whenever I did she changed the subject and became slightly more formal and aloof.

'Did he mention the grey messengers?' she asked me.

The previous day he had been obsessed with 'grey messengers'. He had written notes on the subject on the backs of playing-cards. She had picked up several from the floor of his room. But when she had offered them to him he had dismissed her with a wave.

When I showed an interest in these notes, she unearthed them from the litter bin and put them on the tablecloth next to my plate. I started to match the fragments by turning them over. There were four cards: all queens, numbered 1–4. Above a golfing scene, the blue sky on the back of each card was blackened with Rampick's minute handwriting.

On the first, a queen of clubs, he had written 'A royal footman in the courtyard. I recognize the grey livery.' On the second, a queen of spades 'The same grey messenger. Why is he waiting?' On the third, a queen of hearts, 'The grey messenger is there again. I cross myself.' On the last, a queen of diamonds, 'The grey messenger has gone. I was about to write there is *almost* no sign of him.'

'Yet another of his manias,' she said. ('Not significant' her tone implied.)

On the last card there was also some even tinier writing. Miss Rampick silently brought a magnifying-glass from the sideboard when she saw me squinting to read it.

It looked like 'The Jesuit's chocolate'.

Then she made a remark, meant as a joke, that seemed to me very perceptive about her brother's 'grey messengers'. She said: 'Perhaps he was referring to the snow.' Last week's snow had melted at the beginning of the week, then there had been another snowfall followed by the gradual thaw which was still continuing.

I described the dreams I had had recently about her brother as the Man in the Iron Mask and the apparent awakenings which proved to be continuations of the dreams. My remarks were received with the indifference that the mention of dreams usually evokes in a listener. Probably also she was letting me know that once again I had made the heinous mistake of talking about her brother's delusion as an interesting subject that merited detailed examination like a literary text when it was quite simply a morbid growth, something that it ought to be possible to remove, to cut away.

'I'll have to be going,' I told her, determined to go, but conscious that it was still quite early.

Just at that moment the phone rang. This gave me the opportunity to thank her rather incoherently and hurriedly for her hospitality and say that I would let myself out.

I closed the door gently just as Miss Rampick's warmer telephone voice indicated that she had recognized the caller. From upstairs Rampick was calling out or talking to himself. From the foot of the stairs I tried to decide if the words (I could not make them out) were being uttered in an imperative tone or had the more even flow of a monologue. It was not easy to decide. There were frequent pauses but between the pauses the voice was low and unemphatic. I set off twice down the hall to the front door. Finally I started to mount the stairs as silently as possible.

The door of the attic was ajar.

Rampick was sitting up in bed, holding an imaginary book from which he was reading a description of his surroundings.

'All the window embrasures are walled up except two. At these there are iron bars . . .'

Now and then, during the lengthy description of his dungeon, he lifted and turned his head gravely as though checking his surroundings against the inventory of objects he was reciting.

'Scrawls of charcoal and red chalk on the whitewashed walls . . .'

Suddenly he broke off. In clipped tones, in a strident pettish, high-pitched voice, he said:

'Is this a prison or a local hospital? Is it an asylum or a home for fallen women? Whip the bedlams! Make them bleed!'

His face registered anger, then frenzy. All his limbs began jerking, threshing about. His head rolled from side to side.

I backed away, terrified.

I was still shaking when I reached the living-room door, still treading softly, endeavouring to make no sound that might alert the madman above (a gentle madman no longer) and increase his violence.

Miss Rampick hadn't heard the door open. One bulging cheek visible, her torso twisted, in an ungainly, almost grotesque position, she slouched in front of the fireplace. A biscuit (I can't think of the name*) protruded from her lips. She had picked up the clock from the mantelpiece and was in the process of winding it.

I was inclined to slip away unnoticed. Apart from the embarrassment she might feel at being surprised in an unfeminine, slovenly pose, simply her self-absorption and her evident certainty that she was unobserved, made me hesitate to speak. (She might scream, she might bite her tongue or drop the heavy time-piece.) And my mind was made up when this toad-faced thin little woman suddenly clasped the clock to her not at all noticeable bosom.

I withdrew quickly a second time and left the house.

* I was being disingenuous when I wrote this. I knew perfectly well that it was a bourbon biscuit. (Unfortunately) Not a symbolic detail but a fact. Trivial examples of life imitating art abound. If ever I notice the name on a beer wagon it is certain to be delivering Vaux beers.

CHAPTER NINE

I was so flustered and overwrought that I nearly walked over the dead cat across the street. By the light of a street-lamp I could see it clearly enough. I fancied that what I had earlier taken to be paper-chains were, in reality, fragments of playing-cards. I bent down to get a closer look. Normally this would have been an unthinkable thing for me to do.

Hearing footsteps approaching, I hurriedly walked away without satisfying myself as to what precisely it had been that was scattered over the animal's corpse. But I was ashamed (evidently my shame was greater than my curiosity) that any-one should imagine I was scrutinizing the dead animal out of sadistic interest.

I did not know the time of the next train. Before I got to the station I was feeling guilty at having left Miss Rampick alone with a madman whose paroxysms had unnerved me. Miss Rampick's own eccentric behaviour I had already decided was simply another manifestation of strain. And anyway, to a certain extent, the sanest people act crazily when alone. For some reason I couldn't convince myself that the same logic might apply to Rampick's behaviour.

I remembered with alarm the episode in Rampick's 'Man in the Iron Mask' diary where he had thrown a knife at the witch's back. The memory of his contorted features, the way he had threshed about on the bed, the impression of a dangerous lunatic that he had never given me before, totally effaced my formed conception of a sensitive man afflicted with a distinguished, idealized form of madness.

I now saw Rampick under the double aspect represented by the presiding deities at the gates of old Bedlam, the massive figures representing 'Melancholy Madness' and 'Raving Madness'.

I rang Miss Rampick from a phone box near the station, and

told her I had heard her brother talking to himself as I came away.

She told me not to worry unduly about him. What he had been doing when I heard him was probably reading aloud from his invisible book. She often caught him doing that. Had I not noticed that he himself always spoke in complete sentences like a book?

Two days later I was back once more at Blackhorse Terrace. My fears for the woman's safety, with a violent madman in the house, who appeared to hate her even when he was generally calm and courteous, had pricked my conscience. If I had put off returning for another day I would have sunk back into my usual lethargy and might never have gone back.

I think Miss Rampick was perturbed and mystified at seeing me again so soon. It was a Saturday morning. I had come early, believing there was less chance that she would be out. In fact she had her hat and coat on and was just about to go shopping.

She was sure her brother would be pleased to have another visit from me. She had brought him a scrap pad. This morning he seemed reasonably cheerful. The other evening she had said that lack of company, stubborn uncommunicativeness, lack of a 'desire' for company, had had a pernicious effect on Rampick. Now she said that even before his obsession took hold of him, he had led the narrowest life imaginable. (This sounded like Brenda berating me for never wanting to take her out.) Another face could only do him good.

Without any apparent hesitation, she left me alone in the house with her brother. She must have been convinced of my honesty.

I delayed going up to see Rampick. As Miss Rampick was leaving I had moved towards the stairs as though I were going to see him straight away. But when the outer door had slammed I went into the living-room.

The snow drift had melted in the back garden. The guttering was still lying there.

On the train that morning it had struck me that during the period when Rampick was living in the flats I had played the part that is common in certain novels where there is always someone — a steward, a young kinsman, an impoverished secretary — who is willing to have no life himself and to be fanatically absorbed in the destiny of the chief character, in the smallest detail of his life, to an extent that few people would be content to do. It seemed almost incredible in my case: I was so noticeably self-centred in other ways. Brenda used to complain that I would never do anything to please her unless it was something I also wanted to do myself. And yet I had taken the sort of interest in Rampick that, according to my former philosophy, no one in real life would take, except perhaps a biographer, with an advance from his publisher.

The character in a novel who lives such a life of disinterested curiosity in the progress of the hero I always regarded as a blatant device, an obvious surrogate for the novelist. The only fanatically interested party was the novelist himself and he was fanatically interested in the elaboration and completion of his fiction.

Now at least I had proved to myself that such a person could exist. I still doubted that his passionate curiosity in the affairs of the hero would survive until the dénouement because my own interest in Rampick was flagging. The avid curiosity, that had been extraordinarily keen while he was living in the flats, had diminished considerably.

His madness had originally fascinated me. But since I had got to know the sister better my admiration for Rampick had waned. Miss Rampick was set on delivering him from his illusion with the best of motives. She had made me feel that I had been in danger of succumbing to the temptation of following Rampick into another, imaginary, sphere of life. Perhaps his ability to transform the data of the real world was a knack that I could learn by observation and imitation. Perhaps madness *was* catching.

I had considered Miss Rampick to have been subject to her own therapeutic illusions, such as the illusion that Rampick could be instantly liberated from his fixed idea by a large enough dose of common sense administered at the right psychological moment. It was a large gap in my understanding that I had not yet had an opportunity to observe Rampick and his sister in any kind of direct confrontation. I had not observed her methods of attack. I had not observed his defensive strategies, nor his counterattacks.

In general, though, I was moving now towards Miss Rampick's position, her impatience with the details of her brother's madness. Was there an antidote to the poison that had infected his mental processes? Could the poison be neutralized? I had a prejudice similar to Miss Rampick's, a fear and distrust of psychiatry and psychiatrists.

I left the living-room and toiled up to the attic. Rampick was in bed. Both dormer windows were closed yet the noise from outside was deafening. Lying back on his pillow Rampick made a wry mouth at the window on the front.

'I would give the cross of Saint Louis to the man who would rid me of those pests,' he murmured.

In the normally peaceful street teenagers were kicking a tin can and bellowing. One youth in particular seemed possessed by a vicious and hysterical, almost maniacal passion unnerving to hear.

The boys moved further along the street.

Rampick's mood lightened as soon as the noise had diminished. Smiling, he asked me if the 'chimneypot cat' was still there. Amused by my bewilderment, he made a gesture towards the window at the back. When I looked there was indeed a black cat sitting erect and stiff in the precise spot where you might expect a small chimney to be on the steep roof of the kitchen outhouse.

He asked me for news of the court. Well acquainted with my habitual rustiness of speech, he forestalled my half-audible muttering with a confident: 'Is it true then that the Italian Players have been dismissed for their mockery of Scarron's widow?'

Not expecting or needing any reply he launched into an extended monologue.

'I wonder what filthy stories my brother likes to hear at his *levée* these days? Tales of seduced nuns, the daughters of dukes, giving birth in squalid taverns? Anecdotes of the incredible

debauched de Wateville? Mysteries? The mystery of the black
nun? The ghost in the forest of St Germain?'
　He paused.
　'The King always liked to hear and to talk of mysteries.'
　He paused again significantly.
　'*With one exception.*'
　. . .

　'But perhaps even that story he no longer suppresses. What
harm is there, what danger nowadays, almost in a new century,
in mentioning yet another madman shut up for his follies?
Restrained for the protection of his fellow men like that unfortunate Chevalier who had fits and drew his sword at balls
and receptions, lunging at fire-screens and duchesses, hazard-
tables and royal gamesters indiscriminately.'
　. . .

　'Perhaps he makes a joke of his masked prisoner. And
threatens his impudent daughters with an Iron Headpiece if
they refuse to bridle their tongues.'
　. . .

　'Do not look at me so pityingly! I know what date it is. I know
what changes have taken place. And I was only pretending to
have forgotten, my taciturn friend, that the King is pious these
days. No coarse jokes. No malicious gossip. Nothing but
religious plays and religious persecutions. I know all this. . . .
By the way, is poor Mme de Guyon still imprisoned here? . . .
Every night, even after curfew, through the wall, I hear the
most abominable nasal psalm-singing by that wretched weaver
in his imaginary conventicle. He was on the island with me. He
is here too . . .'
　With violent emphasis, apparently spontaneous venom,
Rampick added: 'You know his mind has gone. All he can think
about is religion.'
　Here was my first opportunity to interrupt his monologue:
'Are you talking about the Protestant, the weaver, or your
brother?' I stammered.
　Rampick softened at this interjection.
　'Louis has chosen a strange time in which to become pious. I

am convinced that God has lost interest in man in this secular age.

'Just imagine,' he continued, 'what future ages will think of us on the evidence of the portraits of outstanding personages, the statesmen, generals, churchmen of our time? We will seem to them to have been a race apart, a rascally, despicable race of pock-marked, hook-nosed villains. Our murderers' eyes. Our ravishers' mouths. Our vicious horsefaces framed by horsehair. A calculating and coarse breed of men. Plotters. Casuists. Inquisitors. Judges. All driven by the mercantile spirit. All stirred by swinish lusts. Mendacious. Intolerant. Malignant. Hypocrites!'

Suddenly he became calmer. He smiled sardonically.

'I nearly split my sides when I saw the caricature of my great brother that the English made when he declined the prospect of a pitched battle with the Prince of Orange. Beating the retreat on his drum. 'King Louis and his Seraglio'. Louis, the periwigged drummer boy. Louis the fearless. Louis the glorious. . . . So brave that whenever he has a pain in his big toe. . . . or a grosser place . . . or his son, the true Prince, has over-eaten . . . Quick! Send for Fagon! Send for Felix! Order the young ladies of St Cyr to go down on their knees! Such a commotion that word of the panic soon reaches the fishwives of *Les Halles* who straight away troop to the Palace to wail at the gates! For their loyal concern, their reward a guided tour of the state rooms and presents from their royal masters . . .

'Good Bontemps', he mimicked in a feigned languid drawl, 'scatter our largesse!'

He resumed in his normal voice.

'When Louis caned the footman he had caught pocketing a biscuit, his head bursting with the intelligence he had just been given of the Duke de Maine's cowardice, you must understand it was his own cowardice he was caning, not merely chagrin at the army's contempt for his favourite bastard.'

For a time he fell silent. Oblivious of his surroundings, he blinked thoughtfully, critically, at an invisible prospect.

What he said next I was unprepared for, although I had, in a way, foreseen it. Earlier I had mentioned the likelihood of

Rampick having read *The Memoirs of d'Artagnan*. Without referring to the author by name he now demonstrated that he had read him.

'I have heard,' began Rampick softly and hesitantly (his voice quavered as if from nervousness and from uncertainty as to how he was going to proceed and be received) 'that as well as madmen and quietists, there is a professional scribbler lodged somewhere within these walls. Soldier and author. Brave and disreputable soldier. Wholly disreputable author.

'I have heard that this fellow is currently at work counter-feiting the unedifying history of our friend d'Artagnan which he hopes to publish abroad. In the Low Countries. The United Provinces. At the Hague.'

'I know the man,' I said.

'Then you will know,' continued Rampick, 'that he is the author of all those spurious memoirs and political testaments of Rochefort and Colbert and Louvois and most recently the spy, Jean Baptiste de la Fontaine whom he met within these walls.'

'M. Courtilz de Sandras,' I remarked as naturally as possible — but my pronunciation was so peculiar that it seemed unlikely that the name fell recognizably on his ears. (The name 'Gatien' I did not even attempt.)

Rampick nodded.

'You may call it a sickly caprice if you like but I have been amusing myself writing episodes in typical memoir style in the first person. I thought you might pass them on to our friend anonymously.'

. . .

'I cannot believe that without some assistance this *scrivano* will have sufficient material . . . genuine material . . . about the captain-lieutenant of musketeers. A few legendary anecdotes, of course. The traditional coarse stories that tapsters and grooms repeat.'

. . .

'But those, together with irrelevant references to great events (that only once or twice touched our hero) will scarcely suffice to fill four volumes. With such a scarcity of material sooner or later revealed to him, I am afraid the rogue will be compelled to make use of his own experiences, transform himself into the notorious Gascon when, with our assistance, he could publish a substantially faithful portrait. A masterpiece. *By his standards.*'

. . .

'I have written a few pages already. Perhaps you could look over them later.'

. . .

'You will observe that I have tried to suit the style to the man, a coarse and flamboyant and vainglorious opportunist as we both know well, as you know in particular, Saint-Mars, however much you may defend him, his memory, out of *esprit de corps.*'

. . .

'I look on it as a kind of diversion from my own Memoirs.'

. . .

'Of course it is a supreme irony that this ignoble hack who lives by impersonating others should be ignorant of my existence: an almost incredible coincidence that the subject of a lifetime for his pseudo-memorializing should be imprisoned in No. 3, Bertaudière. Yet, all unknowing, he continues to squander ink on coxcombs and spies, adventurers and adventuresses no more distinguished than himself.'

. . .

'But an even richer irony, a double irony, do you not think, if the Man in the Iron Mask and his gaoler were to furnish him with information for one of his laboured, mendacious literary performances?'

. . .

'He will never know, hence never regret, how close he came to possessing the key to unlock the Iron Mask. One can say that fortune has been unkind to him but less cruel than she might have been.'

. . .

'Here I have a fair copy of an episode that might entertain you! For all that the incident may be apocryphal, it reveals the man's character and at least is less hackneyed than many others, such as the famous occasion when d'Artagnan, as a spy on the Ormistes, put musket balls through his cloak to convince the rebels he was on their side, and had been in the thick of their fight.'

Rampick fell silent at the sound of a key scratching at the front door key-hole. We both turned to listen, as though the key were unlocking the iron mask. Then we heard the chink of milk-bottles, immutably milk-bottles, that his sister lifted in one by one from the doorstep to stand on the meter cupboard.

Our eyes met.

It seemed a good opportunity to take my leave. But there was no escape until the manuscript of the episode for Courtilz de Sandras, the few pages out of a lined scrap pad, had been put into my hands.

Miss Rampick shook her head at the sight of these pages. And she frowned, without attempting to conceal her displeasure, when I asked for some information about her brother's reading. But this was one occasion when I persisted in the face of her hostility. Rather ungraciously she showed me to the parlour. In one corner a low glass-fronted china cabinet also contained a few books.

The books threw no light on Rampick's obsession. Pocket editions of classics were slightly outnumbered by popular fiction of the Edgar Wallace, Elinor Glyn era, thrillers and contemporary romances rather than historical novels. Only A.E.W. Mason's romance of Sophia Dorothea and Count Königsmark was set in Rampick's favoured century. I had expected Dumas at least; if not those three large format blue-black volumes embellished with gilt fleur-de-lis and a musketeer's head in a tondo, identical to the ones still, unlawfully, in my possession.

Over lunch Miss Rampick admitted to me that all Rampick's personal trash (including some books) was hidden away in a large suitcase in his room. The books I had seen had been her mother's. For the first time she spoke to me about her parents. The father of the Man in the Iron Mask had been a railway porter. Their mother had been a weaver before she married. Later, for many years, she had been a grocery assistant in the market-hall. The father, never a great reader I was surprised to hear, had rented allotments near the park. He had been a keen

amateur musician, playing the flute in a local orchestra and the
piccolo in the military band.

'It would have broken his heart to see the railway station as it
is today,' she said. 'An air raid shelter on one platform. A bus
shelter on the other.'

I made no further efforts to learn more about Rampick's
reading. Miss Rampick would have resented them as futile
attempts at playing the amateur psychologist. I let her enlarge
mainly on her family background, her typist job, changes in the
town, the crowds in town that morning, and sideglances at
more general topics such as the cost of living, strikes, riots, road
accidents, vandalism, the increase in burglaries and attacks on
elderly women.

Miss Rampick had just cleared the table when two workmen
arrived to examine the fallen guttering. She was pleasantly
surprised that they had come on a Saturday. She had known
one of the roof repairers since childhood. With these workmen
she behaved with greater youthfulness and vivacity than I
would have imagined possible.

The three of them went out to discuss the guttering *in situ* on
the back lawn.

Alone in the living-room I felt ignored and neglected. My
situation was made intolerable by the fact that I was so visible
to the workmen. Undecided how to act I remained where I had
been before Miss Rampick had gone to answer the door. From
time to time one of the men would look at me curiously. When I
returned his stare, he would raise his eyes slowly, half-smiling
ironically, to the eaves of the house. Beyond him Sylvia
Rampick, young-old, vivacious-shrewish, smiled and ges-
ticulated.

I read the first sentence of Rampick's impersonation.

'*The greatest mistake that a woman can make is to believe that because
a man values her for one thing, he values everything about her, including
her mind.*'

This seemed like genuine Courtilz de Sandras though I have
never been able to find it in Ralph Nevill's translation. In any
case it was impossible just then to concentrate on Rampick's
pages. After a few minutes, embarrassment sent me upstairs to

keep him company. For once, arriving unannounced, I caught him out of bed. He looked grotesque, Scrooge-like, in a nightshirt, his skinny legs in red slippers.

He was stationed, carefully out of sight, at the back window. I told him the men he could see were workmen. I had made up my mind to restrict my comments, as far as possible, to the literal truth. (What other truth is there?) I would see what effect this had on his conversation. Previously, whenever I had been with him, he had made me feel the real world was more than ordinarily drab. Miss Rampick's conversation over lunch had been extremely prosaic, the sort of conversation I generally only overheard nowadays on buses and trains where I had observed middle-aged men endure the irresistible flow from their wives in stoical silence, their harsh, rigid features masks of despair, their jaws jutting with impotent hatred.

'What is your opinion of the chapter?' Rampick asked me.

I had not had the opportunity to read it, I told him, but was looking forward to doing so.

I added that I had my routine duties to perform. (Already I was romancing.)

I picked up a piece of paper from the floor and handed it to him. It was blank except for one sentence, which suggested Dumas or rather a parody of Dumas in translation: '*A smiling Porthos parried the vicious stroke easily with a joint-stool and continued gnawing at the chicken leg.*'

Suspecting that I had read this, Rampick forestalled any criticism by dismissing it as 'a practice effort'. He was noticeably subdued: this was the closest I had been to seeing him bored and listless. Evidently, even for a monomaniac, there can be occasions when an obsession temporarily loosens its grasp.

He got back into bed. I occupied his former place at the back window. Far below I could see the heads of one of the workmen and Miss Rampick. The second workman was invisible.

I made a direct onslaught on Rampick's entrenched illusion. I told him plainly what the real date was. I said it was a Saturday afternoon. Men were going to football matches, or rather, since this was a town that didn't have a league team, they were watching sport on television. Others were cleaning their cars, gardening, doing household repairs. The rest of the men and the majority of the women and children, so many (I repeated a phrase of his sister's, 'you could walk on their heads') were in town, in the supermarkets, at the old market-hall, looking for bargains at the stalls on the outside market. I prefaced this tedious rigmarole by saying how I had always hated Saturday afternoons, how listless and depressing they were! (Also how unreal in my recital!)

Rampick gave no sign of having taken in a word that I said. I spoke from my position at the window, looking round at him at intervals. In the tense silence that followed my words, I became increasingly nervous. Recently I had experienced un-accountable trembling fits and was growing anxious about a tendency for my limbs to jerk spasmodically. My hand, for example, might give a sudden jerk sideways when I was writing or scooping tea into the pot.

Shaking (visibly shaking I imagined) I went over to the door and from there to the stairhead without looking back. Miss Rampick was still in the garden. The occasional volubility of the most taciturn people is astounding. Her companions were looking up and around and laughing, as though liberated from time. The more curious and alert of the workmen (Miss Rampick's age, her life-long friend?) seemed almost hysterical with laughter.

I couldn't believe that I had spoken to Rampick in the way that I had. Because I had felt physically depressed (perhaps also I was suffering from indigestion) I had acted irresponsibly, childishly. I had even said to him: 'Why is it that you don't speak French?'

My talking in this strain had reduced him to total silence. Eventually he had closed his eyes. I went quickly down the stairs and walked back to the station in the rain.

After miles of obscure wet moorland and upland pastures, with an occasional glimmer of white where snow lingered in cuttings and in the ravines of deeply cleft fields, the first lights of the town appeared.

Since I had left the house in Blackhorse Terrace two hours had passed. I was aware of this, yet imagined nothing in the interim had changed: the conversation with the roofers still in progress, Rampick still feigning sleep. In retrospect my role had been akin to that of the assassin in Rampick's second picture, dagger uplifted to send the wounded Athos to his Maker without benefit of the rites of the Church.

CHAPTER TEN

In the night I woke conscience-stricken. My 'guilt' (at the time no other term would have seemed adequate) showed up in stark contrast: black on white. Little by little distinctions blurred. I grew drowsy. Next morning I was wakened by the thud of a heavy package. A mail-order catalogue for Brenda. One of the little tokens that reminded me of her existence from time to time.

I postponed drawing the curtains; I was reluctant to admit the accusing sun. As I stooped to turn on the gas fire, a voice said: 'A garret overlooking the Place de Grève would be worse. Much worse.' It was the frail, lugubrious, languidly emphatic and feebly tenacious voice of *echo de le pensée*. I was too accustomed to it to be alarmed. The voice suggested a tiny wizened creature, the ancient Voltaire in a bagwig whispering in my ear.

Miss Rampick and the roofers had spent an inordinate length of time talking. It was true nevertheless that I should have left a note or gone out into the garden to say goodbye.

What I had said to Rampick was probably no worse than what his sister had said to him countless times. Strangers, in their ignorance, must have caused him equal vexation and anguish on a host of occasions.

His silence, his attempts to feign sleep, probably signified that what I was saying was no longer meaningful discourse but gabble, a rigmarole in a strange uncouth tongue that merely bewildered him. I reproached myself the more because earlier Rampick had taken such obvious pleasure in having someone with him to appreciate his performance. The poor man's pleasure I had terminated brutally on account of a passing mood, a mixture of lassitude and irritability.

It was a long time before I could bring myself to read the pages intended to help Courtilz de Sandras. In the morning I was too confused and disturbed. In the afternoon the sun was too bright. In the evening it was too noisy. Not until after midnight did I penetrate beyond the first sentence.

During the day I was subject to vague illogical thoughts about what I had told him, thoughts that I was too listless to correct and clarify. Why had I been telling Rampick about Saturday afternoon in a provincial backwater, a decaying town of chimneys and derelict mills? What could I have told him that was more revealing about life in the modern world? Where should I have begun?

I had to struggle to remind myself that this was tantamount to accepting the genuineness of Rampick's role. He was not a Time Traveller from the past. He was not Rip Van Winkle. The last thing that he wanted was to be reminded of the existence of the twentieth century. The worst conceivable punishment for Rampick would have been to re-educate and readjust him to contemporary manners and viewpoints. While many people choose to ignore some aspect or aspects of contemporary life (often to retain their sanity), and while the majority prides itself on ignoring history (recent or remote), Rampick rejected *all* of contemporary life in order to maintain his desired delusions. What was close at hand exerted no power over his imagination, or only a power to evoke what had existed centuries ago, or had never existed except in legend and literature. I am aware of the pointlessness of writing like this, I was and am no nearer understanding the *knack* of his insanity, how he could be so attentive to the imaginary, so blind to the real!

From his pages for Courtilz de Sandras I learned nothing new about Rampick except his fondness for pastiche. The massive, rambling, convincing, brutal effect of the original can hardly be simulated in a fragment. The next time that I saw Rampick, he made no reference to these pages. Neither did he refer to my last visit. Miss Rampick had assumed I had left because her brother had insulted me. This would naturally occur to her as the most likely explanation. She had suffered so much herself from his arrogance and 'literary' tirades. It was not until I had received a letter from her, apologetic in tone, not at all rebuking me for my unannounced departure, and I had written one of my rare letters in reply, that I thought at all about visiting the Rampick household again.

On this occasion Miss Rampick seemed jumpy. The house next door had been broken into, and she was talking about having new locks fitted. It struck me that, while the sister was so anxious about security, the brother imagined himself surrounded by walls 10–12 feet thick, windows defended by three successive gratings, and iron-studded doors secured with iron bars. (In Dumas's *Celebrated Crimes* I had read of the cone-shaped embrasures in a Bastille cell 'growing narrower and narrower towards the outer surface of the walls where they were not six inches across and were guarded by very close iron gratings'.

Rampick's latest preoccupation was to look for reasons why he had been transferred to the capital after so many years in remote fortresses. The little that he said to me that day bore on this question. How to reconcile the handsome treatment he had received on the Island of Sainte Marguerite, his spacious quarters there, with his present cramped and dirty conditions? ('Dirty' was his own distortion of the truth. However the attic was certainly cramped by comparison with his flat in Ruskin House.) Why had the status of the masked prisoner altered?

He also complained of a smell in his room. I assumed he meant the smell caused by an aerosol air-freshener. I racked my brains for a term that would be acceptable to him. Finally I remembered 'oil of rosemary'. With a certain pride, I added the information that it was a defence against the plague. Impatiently Rampick insisted that the smell was nothing like Queen of Hungary water — it was the prison smell he was referring to, a smell compounded of damp, stale air and vermin. He smiled, however, as the ludicrous notion occurred to him ('ludicrous' was the word he used) that perhaps he had been conveyed the length of the kingdom while his quarters in the south were freshened, just as Louis vacated Versailles for six weeks every year while the Palace was cleansed and the foul air changed.

'You see in me the ruins of something much more nobly planned than you,' he said to me in a majestic drawl. Doubtless he did not intend to be offensive. But it seemed a poor sort of return for my painstaking attempts to humour him. Consequently I left him before I was tempted to repeat the feeble shock-tactics of my last visit.

The next hour I spent with Miss Rampick looking through a shirt-box of family photographs. Photographs of parents, grandparents, uncles, cousins, were in the majority but there were several that featured brother and sister together, a picture of Miss Rampick as a Girl Guide, another of her with a dog like the late Max, and one (unrecognizable) of Rampick at the seaside. I scrutinized this one more than most. Behind the boy a blinding white kiosk, white palings, the entrance to a pier. The boy, eyes narrowed against the sun, was standing, lopsided, wide plaid tie blown out to the left, one shirt-sleeved shoulder much lower than the other. I saw no pictures of Rampick taken later than his teens.

One of the last was an unflattering likeness in which the youth's eyes were slits, his nose screwed up, his mouth small-rounded, cheeks puffed out as though he were blowing superciliously on some instrument. His sister assured me that this was not some kind of rude grimace. Philip had always hated having his picture taken. The same 'disgusted' and 'fastidious' look, in less extreme form, with the eyes nearly closed, the rounding of the small mouth suggesting haughtiness or prudish recoil, appeared in other snapshots in which the face could easily have been that of a strait-laced old spinster endeavouring to disregard some gross indecency yet unable to conceal her horrified fascination. I was evidently not the only one to have been struck by this resemblance, for the last item passed to me was a cutting from a local newspaper giving the cast of the Grammar School play. Rampick, aged about thirteen, was playing a woman's part, a witchlike figure in Victorian widows' weeds, looking the very image of an outraged maiden aunt. His performance received special mention for its 'astonishing conviction in portraying an old lady' by 'the youngest member of the cast.'

I went upstairs, feeling more light-hearted than I had ever felt in that house. As I mounted the stairs, I overheard that precocious actor, Rampick the Relict, talking or 'reading aloud'. He fell silent when he saw me. Almost jocularly I asked him where the book was that he had been reading from.

At my words Rampick smiled his 'atheist's smile'.

'It is in my head,' he declared and uttered what sounded like a quotation in a tone of mock self-disparagement: 'A dull and affected folio, long forgotten, in defence of monarchy and the rightful King.'

At the time the following incident seemed insignificant. While I was with Rampick I happened to glance out of the rear window. A boy was perched on the high backyard wall near the gate. Since he wore a dark anorak with the hood up and I was (more or less) in Rampick's orbit of illusion, the boy suggested a debauched monk scaling the convent walls to escape to a house of ill fame. I considered mentioning the intruder to my companion. It would be interesting to test if his interpretation agreed with what I imagined he would say. The boy, meanwhile, looked downwards to the right, into neighbouring yards. And then, because he knew he had been seen, or for whatever reason, he hurriedly turned and prepared to get down the way he had come, his gloved hands visible for a second or two before he dropped into the ginnel.

I was in two minds whether to tell Miss Rampick what I had seen. Because she seemed in an unusual state of nerves, I was reluctant to add to her fears. Fleetingly it occurred to me to wonder if the anoraked figure might not have been 'the messenger' whose existence Rampick had recorded on the backs of playing-cards — although the anorak I saw had not been grey. I half decided to mention the boy to Miss Rampick but it went out of my head before I saw her. Later I was inclined to appease my conscience for my forgetfulness by telling myself that in all likelihood his motives had been mischievous rather than criminal.

At the end of this chapter, as a kind of appendix to this part of Rampick's history, I have copied out a self-sufficient episode from Rampick's impersonation of Courtilz de Sandras or, in Rampick's inverted reasoning, his specimen material *for* that author. I consider these pages to be evidence that Rampick was starting to tire of the narrow confines of his Man in the Iron Mask role. It seems to me perfectly natural, and not at all surprising or out of character, that the role of a man of action should appeal (as a refreshing contrast) to the imagination of the meditative, celibate recluse, who lived in a cell of pride rather than humility, but had essentially a conventual life-style. His excessive dislike of d'Artagnan is itself suspect, and suggests a covert admiration for an antithetical type, for the swaggerer who lived according to his father's advice to seek out adventures, the impoverished young Charles de Batz de Castelmore whose panache and impetuosity, and whose equally striking cunning and clear-headedness in circumstances of great risk and danger, made him a byword for dash and gallantry. The frequency of Rampick's allusions to his enemy (often introducing his name on the flimsiest pretexts) testifies to his fascination.

As Rampick himself had stated, these pages were by way of being a relaxation from his memoirs, the bulk of which (mercifully unknown to him) had been destroyed, although, theoretically, the confiscated pages were in my safe-keeping. From Rampick, to assume the identity of d'Artagnan on paper meant that he could indulge a forbidden dream of the delights of an unrestrained and vulgar life; one that he secretly envied, but that his sobriety and moral rectitude rejected. Rampick, the abstemious, merely wrote and imagined, combining 'the resignation of a martyr with the smile of an atheist'.

MATERIAL FOR D'ARTAGNAN'S MEMOIRS

'. . . The greatest mistake that a woman can make is to believe that because a man values her for one thing, he values everything about her, including her mind. When Miladi's maid had me in her power perhaps she did not care (even if she realized) that, as far as I was concerned, she was a girl to whom lechery alone attracted me. But the majority of women are not like her. They wish us to admire their musical or other idle accomplishments, be

they ever so humble. Or at the very least they wish us to admire their skill with a needle or their ability to cook a ragout. . . . Many times I have been approached by the stratagem of a letter sent to me by an unknown woman wishing to make my intimate acquaintance and stating her passion for my appearance and martial qualities (the usual expression is "dying of love for you") in no uncertain manner. If the handwriting has been spidery or I have been feeling exhausted from the rigours of military exercises, or in the grip of my quintan fever, I have not risen to the bait. But on the occasions when I have kept the rendezvous urged upon me (at the Porte St Antoine or Porte St Honoré or perhaps more promisingly in some quiet out-of-the way side street or by-lane in the suburbs) a curtained remise has been inevitably waiting, drawn up against the peeling wall of a hospital or asylum, and inside the carriage has been sitting, if I was lucky, a masked lady (with or without a duenna) who, by her appearance, her hair, her unlined neck, her single chin, and what I could discern of her figure, has been young and apparently agreeable and reasonably fascinating. It is true, as the writer says, that "a wench to please a man does not come dropping down from the ceiling on to his pikestaff as he lies dreaming lustfully on his bed". And if, nine out of ten times, when I have gone to the trouble of keeping a rendezvous, the wear of boot leather and the interruption of a good hour's drinking of the wine of Langon (or a game of billiards) has proved only doubtfully worth the candle, on the tenth occasion the woman has been neither too old, too scraggy, nor too egregiously whorish — and it must be allowed that an impecunious, if well-born, man of the sword like myself cannot afford always to be the irreproachable cavalier — not to satisfy me for a few hours, a few days even, and if the fair letter-writer has the good sense to make a reasonable pretence at modesty (as there is nothing more exciting than virtue and nothing less agreeable than shamelessness) my infatuation may last even longer. This exceptional felicity has been achieved at least three times and it never occurred to me that there may be danger involved in keeping such rendezvous — other than the perils of encountering a pox-ridden toothless old hag or some incurable madwoman from the provinces who had seen me execute a masterly demi-volte on parade and wished me to perform more intimate evolutions with her in bed — until the day that I strolled to keep an appointment arranged by a letter addressed to the "Brave Chevalier from the South" in an unknown woman's hand, a generous woman moreover who promised to bring with her three hundred pistoles as proof of her goodwill. Two coaches were waiting against the walls of a lazaret. I passed by on the other side, trying to glimpse inside without making it too obvious what I was about. At the corner I began whistling and retraced my steps closer to the carriages in the dust of that very squalid street. I stole a quick glance in the first coach but could see nothing in the dusky interior. Passing the second I imagined I glimpsed something and opened the door boldly with an excuse prepared if there should be some mistake. However instead of the rustle of silks and the soft, pliant body of my fair epistoler (hot to be mounted and sluiced) I felt the cold point of a dagger at my throat. There was no woman in the remise only four ruffians in black with broad slouch hats. I was steered to a place between two of the men by the man with the knife, the only one whose face I could see clearly. This man had the bony, yellow, narrow face of the hired assassin; he was the image of one of the most cunning bravoes of Rosnai (whom I knew to have been rotting in his grave for ten years) and I suspected he was one of the reformadoes employed from time to time by the Abbé Fouquet. The man seated next to him, also with his back to the horses, held a pistol aimed at my head as if impatient to salute me with a bullet were I to make the slightest movement. The men on either side of me were also armed with pistols. When I was settled the man facing me twitched the curtains to, then drummed with the pommel of his dagger on the roof of the carriage. No one spoke. Looking from one half-hidden face to another, I decided there was nothing to gain by addressing any of them. Then, as the lumbering coach rolled, the little man facing me smiled, a smile broad as a melon, showing disgusting crooked tobacco-stained teeth. Involuntarily (because I am not by nature long-suffering and if the smile was insulting the stench of his breath was a graver impertinence) I grasped the hilt of my sword when a hand "as large as a shoulder of mutton and as dry as that of a man hanged in summer" covered mine while the pistol in his other hand was raised, apparently ready to smash my fingers if I resisted, so that I had no alternative but to loosen my grip on the hilt, at the same time relaxing my entire body, which the men on either side of me must have felt because they seemed to relax also. The little man smiled again but less broadly this time and ran his finger along the blade of the dagger with the rouelle guard. All this while the carriage was moving rather slowly but without halting and I tried to work out where we were going but soon found this was impossible except that, as we had not turned right around, I was fairly confident that we were not travelling out of the city. When the little man lifted the curtain I saw that we were about to enter the Bastille. I looked at his face and at the faces of his companions. The curtain fell back. I began to sweat in earnest. As soon as we came within the walls of the fortress, the members of my escort visibly relaxed and, at a signal from their leader, concealed their weapons. For his part he smiled in what seemed intended to be an amiable fashion and put away his knife. The coach came to a halt in a corner of a small yard and the little man, with newly acquired courtesy, bowed and led the way to an open door. There were some damp orange sheets hanging from a drying-line which we were compelled to struggle through to get to this door. The rest of the escort remained behind in the carriage while their leader and I waited in an unfurnished room just to the right of the entrance way. Our view of the courtyard was obstructed by the sheets which threw an angry glare on the whitewashed walls. I reflected that the governor, my 'friend' François de Besmaux, was at Fontainebleau and his underling was an individual I was unacquainted with. But Mme Besmaux I knew (although relations between us were not cordial) and usually she did not accompany her husband anywhere or indeed go out except to a church close by. Evidently it was high time that I took a strong line with this carved monkey of a bravo and I had turned to him in a threatening manner when he forestalled me with yet another of his insufferable smiles and said: "I apologize, Chevalier, for the discourteous treatment you have received at our hands but our instructions were to bring you here without fail. Explanations were forbidden and we knew that there was no trifling with a man from Béarn, such a notable swordsman. The zeal of my comrades and myself was merely an indication of the fear your name inspired in us." At this juncture, while he was watching me closely to decide if his words had mollified me at all, a bashful, hesitant fellow made his entrance. This was obviously not a guard or turn-key (he looked more like a clerk or personal servant) and he bade me very politely, even abjectly, to follow him up a narrow turngrece. I ascended the steps in silence, without haste, curious rather than afraid or aggrieved, my hand on my sword which had not been taken from me, the clerk two steps ahead of me, the bravo bringing up the rear and with the same irritating reassuring smile contorting his ugly features whenever I glanced back, which was frequently, at each turn of the stair. Mme Besmaux was waiting in the first room we entered. The servant and the bravo disappeared at once. Mme Besmaux wore the famous mask with a large face-cloth that I had been told her jealous husband had recently made her wear continually in the prison, but I could not fail to recognize her by her general appearance which was far from unpre-possessing. From the very first moment it was clear to me that I was not the man she was expecting and that her dangerous (insane) plan to become better acquainted with someone she had admired from afar had misfired and disastrously so, since, if Besmaux and myself were not exactly David and Jonathan, our acquaintanceship was of long duration and the daughter of Pluvinel had shown herself far from amiable to me in the past so that she could not reasonably expect a favour from me as a matter of course. We were both dumbfounded, at a loss for words, and probably from embarrassment (and relief, too, that such sinister proceedings should have ended in this way) I began to laugh heartily, at that moment, too, realizing which of my comrades it must be, a Chevalier who until recently lodged with me, a Béarnais from Pau, a regular fire-eater and good companion but unfortunately tainted by the Italian vice and consequently not at all interested in the fair sex, that poor Mme Besmaux was so extravagantly enamoured of . . .'

The above episode represents about one third of what Rampick had written. He could not have expected me to have had access to the original — the original, that is, in English guise — of the author he had been imitating. It may be convenient here to mention a remark Rampick made about Courtilz de Sandras that copying out the above has just reminded me of. 'The cumulative effect', he told me, 'will almost certainly be that of a man damning himself out of his own mouth and, incidentally, there will be abundant opportunities to cast doubt on the gloriousness of his master.' Rampick had also suggested that I should imply that the material passed to the memoir-writer was found among d'Artagnan's papers. The fact that I (as Saint-Mars) had served with d'Artagnan in the Grey Musketeers should vouch for their authenticity. 'The handwriting?' I had countered, to which Rampick had reasonably replied that it was unlikely that my prisoner was familiar with d'Artagnan's hand. 'D'Artagnan was a man of the sword, not M. Colbert or the President Toussaint.' The project, as I have already said, was never referred to again. I imagine this was because of my 'rebellion' later the same day. On every occasion that I visited

Rampick after his accident I lived in dread of him bringing up the subject of the writings Miss Rampick had destroyed while he was in hospital. You may remember that she had told him these were in my possession. For this reason, after making copies, I returned to Miss Rampick the originals of the 'diary' and the episode just quoted, with the thought that these would at least be something that could be returned to Rampick if he suddenly became distressed and agitated over the absence of his manuscripts.

II

CHAPTER ELEVEN

The dreamer retires to his apartment, shuts out
the cares and interruptions of mankind, and
abandons himself to his own fancy. . . . He is at
last called back to life, by nature, or by custom,
and enters peevish into society, because he cannot
model it to his own will.
'The Rambler', No. 89, SAMUEL JOHNSON

The situation in which I next found myself was so completely new to my experience that, by contrast, I seemed to have been comparatively light-hearted, smiled on by fortune, until that moment. After the initial shock and the strain of coming to terms with the new situation, I was reluctant to make the slightest extra effort. The reasons were very far from being the old sluggishness and that peaceful resigned sense of futility that from time to time used to paralyse my will.

Is there a name for people who dread the process of self-justification? A 'Cordelia complex'? In a civilized society, among honest men, should the truth not be self-evident? Any attempt to give a good account of oneself is an exercise in vanity, in special pleading, in duplicity.

However, in my new, atrocious circumstances, I soon recognized the necessity of making an effort to persuade and convince others. Only it made me nervous. There was a sense of pressure on me, an alien grip that never relaxed its hold. It distorted whatever I said or wrote. It even distorted the half-formulated thoughts in my head. I lived continually in the presence of an invisible judge. My handwriting became spidery. I felt I was on a tightrope (I saw everything in exaggerated, melodramatic terms).

Doubt (and 'doubt' is an understatement) had been thrown on much of what I had written. I will explain the circumstances in due course. Here I will give a few brief examples of what I mean.

One example (admittedly an extreme example) was 'The

Diary of the Man in the Iron Mask' which had been identified as an adaptation of quite a celebrated case history quoted in a standard work on . . . (on delusions, paranoia, I suppose!), I was told that between the wars, during the demolition of a large house (formerly a *maison de santé*) on the outskirts of Paris, workmen had discovered a rolled up manuscript among the rubble of a chimney wall. For a long time the identity of the author was not known. The author of the standard work refers to the paranoid 'diarist' as 'R'. The manuscript, it seems, is now thought to have been written by one Constantin Mahalin, poet son of a banker. The poet, who believed himself to be the masked prisoner, had been a patient in various private asylums. As a final gesture in 1903 he had committed suicide on the two-hundredth anniversary of the death of the Man in the Iron Mask. Before the discovery of the manuscript this act was the young Frenchman's one claim to immortality. According to Dr Scullard (about whom I will have more to say later), his suicide was referred to by various writers, particularly by surrealists (or was it existentialists?) in works that I am afraid were totally unknown to me.

I was somewhat reluctant to take Dr Scullard's word for the closeness of the resemblances between the texts, but if this was the case the plagiarism was Rampick's not mine. I had transcribed the pages in good faith, the dupe of Rampick in this respect as, apparently, in others.

My testimony that Rampick always acted in character as a seventeenth-century prisoner was somewhat discredited by a pocket diary, four years old, found in the living-room sideboard. This was the only specimen of Rampick's writings found anywhere in the house. Only one passage mentioned the Man in the Iron Mask. It contained modern allusions as well.

The passage was as follows:

Marcel Proust died today, on the birthday of Louis Daguerre (considering his disdain for photographic realism this seems ironic) and the day before the death of the Man in the Iron Mask (another legendary immured figure whose confines in his last years had grown narrower). The birthday of the masked prisoner (if you discount the twin princes of legend) is, of course, conjectural.

The passage overflowed from the 18th to the 19th of November.

The handwriting in the diary was exactly the same as the handwriting I was used to from his memoirs, etc.

Doctors who had treated Rampick in the past claimed to have no suspicions of any tendency to delusions of grandeur. According to their files, his problems were much less esoteric. He had a history of sexual offences against young boys, but he was regarded as apparently no longer in danger, possibly even cured. It was some years since he had been charged with any offences; at least five years since he had undergone any treatment.

After the disappearance of Rampick and his sister and the discovery on their premises of a badly injured youth, it seemed as though I was the only person available to help the police with their enquiries. (The circumstances I will soon describe.) In future I was determined that everything I wrote would be distinguished by an absence of any kind of decoration. I would extirpate all those evocative touches that suggested fabrication. At the risk of appearing to harp on trivial matters, I was very sensitive to the grave doubts that had been thrown on my conception of the truth. It was put to me that from beginning to end my narrative was a tissue of falsehoods, the episodes attributed to Rampick being just as much a product of my imagination as my costume-piece dreams and all the rest. Apparently no other witness could be found to support my accounts of the missing man's delusion. Few people were aware of his existence. One neighbour only three doors away was adamant in his belief that Miss Rampick's mentally handicapped brother had been in an institution all his adult life.

It did me no good to have to confess to the police that the three examples of original writing by Rampick that I had incorporated into my narrative only existed now in my handwriting. The originals were not found at No. 1 Blackhorse Terrace. By a sort of contagion the doubts cast on the authenticity of these portions spread to the authenticity of my accounts of Rampick's conversation. It was accepted that Rampick was not normal. The question then was what of my own status? What if I had been the leading spirit in the charades I described, instead of occupying a supporting role as I had claimed?

The fact that nothing relating to Rampick's obsession was found in the house was inexplicable. More than anything it put me in a panic. I had been the first caller at the house. I could throw no light on the Rampicks' disappearance. I had no information to give about the presence of the youth with head injuries. All I could tell the authorities was tied up with my unsupported testimony about Rampick's paranoia. My object in disclosing the manuscript to the police was to spare myself the trouble of endless explanations. The attitude to it varied. On one occasion Superintendent Bradley called it 'a gigantic red herring designed to obscure your real relationship with the missing couple'. To intimidate me still more he struck the folder containing my manuscript with his own gigantic red fist.

Other circumstances, fortunately, did not incriminate me: the distance I had to travel to get to the Rampicks' house, and the fact that I had no car and could not drive, were in my favour.

I did not retract anything of what I have written so far in this narrative except insofar as all reminiscences contain an element of distortion and heightening for the sake of readability. I am basically rather literal-minded and sensitive to accusations of distortions in memory and observation. There are inevitably details in the foregoing narrative that have imaginative overtones. There are incidents that I have more or less consciously added to or simplified, for effect. The 'truth' of my dreams and reveries I can only affirm. Basically, however, in police terms, in court-room terms, I insisted that the narrative was truthful. Rampick suffered from the delusion I described. His sister knew of the delusion. She gave me to understand that it was a condition of some duration. About her truthfulness in general, as well as in this particular, I was beginning to have serious doubts. In an emotional outburst, after prolonged harassment, I told the Superintendent that I had no positive *proof* the Rampicks were brother and sister. They might be man and wife, lovers, ex-lovers, or transvestites. A great deal might have been concealed from me. The more I thought about it the more naive and gullible I seemed to have been; more than ready to see what I wanted to see, and to hear what I wanted to hear.

At times Superintendent Bradley seemed impressed by my sincerity and consistency. More often he was all too obviously suppressing impatience over the fact that most of the information I had given him about the Rampicks had been of no practical value. He would obviously have been glad to exchange it all for a single clue to the couple's whereabouts.

The woman who had 'abducted' Rampick and brought him to the flats could not be traced. I gave the police as complete a description of her as possible. In fact there was little to add to what I have written. It would have been a sort of corroboration if I had mentioned Rampick's obsession to Brenda, but at the time it would have seemed a cruel breach of confidence and anyway would have immediately had the consequence of my sharing the limelight of ridicule with Rampick. Brenda would have thoroughly enjoyed the harm she could have caused me by spreading the word that I was the intimate friend of the local lunatic.

When Brenda had been frightened by Rampick's face at the window, I had been under the impression that on this occasion at least he had been wearing a mask. But in Brenda's statement to the police there was no mention of a mask. It was a horrible grimace that had alarmed her. I was correct in my assumption that no one else in Ruskin House had any knowledge of Rampick's mania.

My literary efforts certainly increased police suspicions about me. I am not suggesting that the police were especially interested in how far they believed my version of the missing recluse's obsession. It was my veracity in general that was in question. (My veracity and my soundness of mind.) Bradley wanted to know if I intended to pass my narrative off as non-fiction or fiction. Candidly I didn't know how to answer him. I had had vague thoughts of publication but only as a possibility at a much later date. I had rewritten and polished certain chapters. Did this constitute an intention to burden library shelves? If certain passages showed a kind of self-indulgence perhaps more appropriate to fiction, in my own mind the dividing line between reminiscence and fiction has never been altogether clear.

It seemed to me that the danger to avoid most, if I decided to continue with this narrative, was the danger of adopting the staccato, exaggerated, self-incriminating style usually found in statement by suspects. A style that is the reverse of persuasive, that reeks of bad nerves and a bad conscience!

The fact that I felt myself to be a suspect (an accessory of some kind) made it hard to write calmly. I postponed writing for several weeks, hoping that in time the feeling of strangeness would pass off and I would recover my equilibrium. In the early stages neither alcohol nor even tranquillizers helped me.

I had been surprised how shrewd the police could be in their attitude to a literary composition from a non-literary point of view. (From a literary point of view, with the exception of the highly intelligent Inspector Dixon, their comments were asinine.) For example, they pounced on my hapless confession that I had a poor memory for recording conversations. Surely, they said, this was contradicted by other passages where I had apparently reproduced Rampick's conversation word for word. My defence (feeble enough) was that these passages showed touches of 'doctoring'. They concluded that such 'doctoring' could only destroy the value of a piece of writing as a document. They were unconvinced by my arguments that essentially the conversations were as I had reproduced them.

There were many other instances of this kind of thing. It is no exaggeration to say that the favourite police method of interpretation is to take a sentence or even a phrase out of context and read into it a sinister meaning. With obvious relish they produced the unfortunate phrase 'the accusing sum'. Why 'accusing'? I respond very badly to questioning of this sort. I stammered. I tried to explain it away as a poetic touch. I mentioned the remorse I had felt after my malicious, ill-tempered conversation, attempting to undermine Rampick's 'Card Kingdom of Fancy'. The police showed the same impatience as Rampick's sister at the first sign of 'flowery' talk. To attempt to put the record straight, in defiance of the average

man's simplifications, the truth is that I have always felt uncomfortable on a day of splendid weather. My deepest nature is
apheliotropic. The sun makes me feel an outcast. I am found
wanting in some way. Practically speaking I find it impossible
to know how to take fullest advantage of a spell of good weather.
The common expression, 'It's a sin to stay indoors on a day like
this', the kind of folk wisdom forever on the lips of old women on
their way to the shops, I treat with deadly seriousness. It
reinforces the feeling of guilt the sunshine gives me. The sun,
incidentally, exposes the dust and dirt in my flat, the ladder of
dust down the wardrobe mirror, cobwebs on the ceiling, dead
flies on the chipped window-sill, the greyness of my lace
curtains untouched since Brenda left. The sun also emphasizes
my sense of personal ugliness and gaucherie. Despite the vivid
evidence of my eyes, and the fact that I feel myself to be an
object of derision and condemnation (*mocked* by the sun,
reproached by the sun, *accused* by the sun,) I consider myself
essentially out of reach of its splendours. Broken glass, an
explosion of light on waste ground; cars stacked and gleaming
like thick-waisted coloured bottles in a parking lot; the gilt
weather-vanes, winged arrows glistening above the pinnacles of
the parish church tower; these things I observe, but the items in
my surroundings that I feel kinship with are the desolate
massive immutable presences that even the sun cannot
transform, such as the damp old walls of the mill with the
Victorian hatter's antiquated slogan in giant lettering that was
visible from the island of Sainte-Marguerite. And how is it that,
at the same time that I am dazzled by the sword blade of the
sun, I also feel as if I were chained in some dank and lightless
dungeon underground — with all the weight òf the earth
pressing down on me, my precise vision of such a dungeon being
the cellars beneath the old derelict Co-op outfitters on the main
road?

'Flowery' and wiredrawn as the above might seem I know it is
more adequate in conveying the truth of what I meant by
'accusing sun' than the brief, sensible, fundamentally evasive
replies I was coerced into uttering at the time. As regards the
police, if I had been mad enough to elaborate orally on the lines

of the above, a knowing look would have appeared, even in the eyes of the urban and cultured Inspector Dixon. The same look I had already encountered in Dr Scullard's eyes.

Dr Scullard, of course, is licensed to be super-subtle and outrageous in his theories. As a psychiatrist he has the protection of his jargon, his professional status. At first I was not clear whether he was the same psychiatrist who had treated Rampick a number of years before or a colleague with access to Rampick's files. It was Dr Scullard who identified the plagiarized diary pages after finding them initially familiar. A million to one chance I would have thought. I know nothing of the literature of psychiatry and psychotherapy — their inter-connexions and internecine warfare — nothing of their case histories except Freud's studies of 'Dora' and 'Little Hans'. I imagine university stack-shelves groaning with the photo-lithographed pages of the proceedings of conferences held in all the capitals and university cities of the world, arranged by longer and longer Roman numerals.

In the search for clues to the whereabouts and state of mind of the youth's attacker (sex fiend? gentle provoked paranoiac?) my poor manuscript was subject to greater scrutiny than it would ever have received at the hands of generations of literary critics. In a way this flattered me even though I realized that such scrutiny excluded appreciation. Doggedly they sifted through it. 'Rather obvious and rhetorical speculations,' according to Dr Scullard. 'Icing on the cake,' according to Superintendent Bradley. Foolish as this must sound, I felt grateful to the authorities for the typescripts they made. The sight of the improved appearance of my manuscript, the ample margins and the wide spacing, gave me considerable satisfaction. It was in honour of the handsome photocopy that I purchased a spring-back binder so that I could read it like a book. At the same time I was sure the manuscript had been an infuriating disappointment to the police in their enquiries, and had been damaging to me, generating suspicion. I felt that whatever the outcome — and frankly, in spite of the bad state of my nerves caused by all the upset, I was not really unbalanced enough to believe that the police were likely to concoct a case against me

— I would never be totally absolved from complicity because of the existence of my dubious manuscript.

CHAPTER TWELVE

I did not discover the badly injured youth. When I arrived at the house, a uniformed constable opened the door. There were detectives everywhere. The boy's name was Andrew Jast. He was well-known to the police. Recently, especially since he had left school, he had graduated from shop-lifting to burglary. He might have been the youth I saw crouching on the backyard wall. I could not positively identify him.

The reason why the police had broken into the house I was not told at first. (Actually an anonymous phone call, a woman's voice.) The boy had been found in Rampick's garret. He had been struck on the back of the head with a blunt instrument. On the day that I walked into the middle of all this, the boy was in intensive care and the police were ready to treat the case as a murder enquiry. I could not stop shaking as I was taken to the police station, to the hospital, back to the house, to my flat (to fetch my manuscript and for the police to question neighbours there), to the police station again. I was interviewed by various police officers, by Superintendent Bradley, Chief Inspector Dixon, Sergeants Flinders and Duano. Later I saw the psychiatrist, Dr Scullard.

At first I seemed to be embroiled in a murder enquiry with the chief suspects nowhere to be found and my own relationship to them at the very least considered 'eccentric and dubious'. However, the injured youth's condition gradually improved and the sense of urgency began to fade. The explanation that Rampick had struck the boy and that his sister was shielding him, afraid that the youth might be dead, had always seemed the most likely. It was unfortunate for me that no close friend or relative could be traced. I was in the unenviable position of being the only person claiming to have an intimate knowledge of Rampick's condition. This seemed to the police an incredible state of affairs in itself. And if I had so much privileged inside knowledge, was it not reasonable to assume that I might know something about the Rampicks' disappearance, or at least where they were likely to have gone?

Mercifully the delirium of the first days did not last. I recovered my equilibrium. I even grew used to police interrogation. As the boy's condition improved, my significance dwindled. My life was returning to normal. Days passed without the telephone ringing. I started to read again.

The last long interview that I had with a policeman was with Chief Inspector Dixon. He called at the flats one morning. The purpose of the visit seemed very largely humanitarian, to reassure me. The injured youth appeared to be well on the way to recovery. He was already uttering threats against the police as well as against Rampick. (At some time he must have seen Rampick although he claimed to have been struck from behind as he entered the attic. He described him as 'that white-faced streak of misery.')

'I don't need to remind you that it is your duty to get in touch with us if you hear from the sister,' Dixon told me.

As on previous occasions, Dixon took a delight in making fun of his superior, the immensely tall and corpulent Bradley. The Superintendent was known to his men as the 'clockwork constable', partly because of his shape and slow deliberate waddling gait and partly because a favourite expression of his was that he only needed to wind so and so up and he could obtain any information he wanted. This reminded me of an occasion when the Superintendent had told me that it wasn't only writers who needed to know what made people tick.

'That's the Superintendent!' exclaimed Dixon, apparently delighted to have another example to add to his store of Bradley phrases.

Dixon handed me a large Numbrian folder. It contained my original, much-corrected, dog-eared manuscript.

'I am afraid some of it is missing,' he apologized, 'but I believe you were given a photostat copy. When I was talking to Dr Scullard the other day he promised to forward to you a copy of that case-history he referred to, the one that resembles Rampick's.'

I must have made a wry face at the mention of the psychiatrist because the Chief Inspector went on to say that, believe it or not, Scullard was a man who improved on closer acquaintance.

'I can understand your prejudice. But from his professional viewpoint there seemed a good deal that was questionable in your account of Rampick's delusion. He thinks your great weakness lies in being too prone to adopt a "disciple's role" '.

I interrupted. 'Does he think I need psychiatric treatment?'

Dixon smiled. 'I don't get the impression that he's anxious to take on extra patients,' he said. 'But let's get back to your friend, Rampick. Dr Scullard reckons that you over-estimated the scope and detail of his knowledge. He drew a comparison with a teacher who may be called upon to teach a subject unfamiliar to him, and only be one lesson ahead of his class. It's the teacher's expertise, his fluency and experience of the world, if you like, that deceives his young pupils into accepting the myth of his superior knowledge.'

I nodded as he paused. The Inspector continued.

'Dr Scullard tells me that he remembers Philip Rampick very well and that he has a much higher regard for his histrionic abilities than for his scholarship. Also he can give more credence to his intention to deceive than to his genuine derangement. Dr Scullard thinks that you cooperated in the illusion more than you imagine.'

'I find it very hard to believe that Rampick's delusion isn't genuine,' I said.

'Well, obviously the doctor can't be sure it isn't either,' Dixon replied. 'He admits it's a puzzle. Still, if Rampick's delusion is genuine your contribution was still of the greatest importance. You colluded with him. You helped him act out his fantasies in a private, protected environment, whether you realized it or not.'

It seemed the police were no nearer discovering the whereabouts of Rampick and his sister. The Inspector brought me up to date with their investigations — or at least with what he considered he could divulge to me. (His apparently irresponsible frankness, I had decided at earlier meetings, was a question of tactics.) According to Dixon there seemed no longer any reason to entertain the least suspicion that I had been involved in a conspiracy. In fact the whole matter could be seen to be quite distinct from Rampick's delusion.

I protested at this. I reiterated what I had told the police previously, that Rampick would have assigned the young burglar to some imaginary role and seen his purpose there as an assassination attempt.

'That's perfectly possible,' Dixon said. 'But it's only your speculation. Any householder, surprised by an intruder, might react with violence. We think he probably struck the youth in self-protection and his sister believed he had killed the intruder. Hence their disappearance.'

The Inspector seemed more sombre than he had been at first.

'I have a good deal of sympathy for them. Lawbreakers never go short of apologists these days. If you were to listen to Jast's parents, and even the probation officer, the lad is overflowing with good intentions yet no amount of sympathetic understanding seems to deter him from his criminal activities.'

'You have given us useful background information,' he told me. 'And I personally deplore the fact that in some quarters your testimony was treated with such a lack of respect. It's the police mind, I'm afraid. We tend to be suspicious-natured because we are lied to so often. I think even the Superintendent realizes it wasn't your fault that you had so little hard information to give us. By the way, we know now why the neighbours knew so little about the couple.'

'Oh, yes!' I said doubtfully.

'Yes,' said Dixon. 'Naturally you assumed, or perhaps the sister suggested, that the house was the family home. You thought they'd always lived there or at least that they'd lived there for a good number of years. Not true, it seems. The fact is that until a couple of years ago the Rampicks lived on the other side of town, in a rather better area, where there's no shortage of people who know a good deal about them.'

'Does anyone support my story?' I asked.

'No. Unfortunately not. But most people agree that Rampick has always been very odd. And notorious, too, of course, because of the cases of sexual assault. Most people think the sister was foolishly protective to her brother. Do you realize she is quite a few years older than Rampick? She more or less brought him up. The parents were separated. The mother left the district.'

'This doesn't agree with what she told me,' I said.

'I'm sorry,' he said. 'But we have dozens of witnesses now.' Dixon carefully stubbed out his cigarette. He shrugged.

I said that to all appearances Miss Rampick was tired of her brother being such a burden to her. All along I hadn't been able to understand why she hadn't called the police. Rampick's attack on the youth ought to have been the last straw, the occasion for her long-deferred decision to have him committed to an institution.

'I'm sure she gave you that impression,' the Inspector said.

Dixon thanked me for the coffee I'd made him. I thanked him for the return of my manuscript and for coming such a long way.

'It's really not so far,' he said. 'It takes less than half an hour by car.'

According to what he said the distance between the two towns was more like twenty than the forty miles I had estimated.

He shook hands with me at the door. I reminded him of the roof repairers, the man who had seemed to be an old friend of Miss Rampick's.

'We haven't traced them. Almost certainly they were cowboys.'

He asked me, smiling, if I had returned the library books yet. I felt myself reddening. I told him I had.

He grimaced at the dust on the landing. Through the open window we could hear church bells although it was a weekday morning.

'I should think it can be very noisy in these flats,' he said. I agreed. I mentioned the motor-cyclists.

A woman was ascending the first flight of steps. She was almost upon us before she noticed the Inspector. I was stunned. Perhaps my face conveyed a warning or Sylvia Rampick was able to recognize a detective, whereas my verbal description of the woman must have conveyed no accurate image to him. Dixon hardly glanced at her. Her face registered nothing. She nodded briefly and continued up the next flight. Dixon grimaced again at the dust like sand in the corners and on the concrete steps, the dust that begrimed the blue-painted stair-rails. He went quickly downstairs with a final wave.

I went back into the flat and watched him from the window. Miss Rampick meanwhile had toiled steadily up to the highest flats. She was beginning her descent as I opened the front door. 'That was Inspector Dixon' I told her. Without saying a word she went through into the living-room.

I repeated what I had said in a louder voice. She looked as though she might be in a state of shock. She seemed obsessively attentive to the tiny brass candlestick on the left-hand side of the gas fire. I looked over her head out of the window. I had no idea what to do next. I asked her if she wanted coffee. Tea? She made no reply. I went into the kitchen all the same. As I filled the kettle I tried to think practically.

When I came back into the living-room I found she had fainted. In the next few minutes I had hammered on the door of the flat across the landing, with no response, and had gone down to the ground-floor flat because I had heard that the woman who had moved in there was a nurse. No one had answered the door. Back in my own flat Miss Rampick, still unconscious, lay in the same position.

I rang the police, the number I had been told to ring, stammering and gulping my words. As I watched for the police and the ambulance I noticed Brenda hanging washing out in a far corner of the courtyard. An old friend of hers, an Italian called Mauvilli, was talking to her as she pegged the clothes on the drying-line. Brenda was wearing jeans, a pink blouse, a red turban. She must have been aware of me at the window because Mauvilli turned and gave a prolonged stare in my direction. Another woman joined them, a coloured girl who always wore a sheepskin jacket. I was watching this group when the police car appeared. An ambulance arrived a few moments later.

It seemed inevitable that Inspector Dixon would recognize

the woman who had passed us on the stairs. I had recourse to the vainest of hopes according to the formula that 'whatever one fears most rarely happens'. Dixon recognized her at once. He eyed me coldly. I was taken to the hospital. After a while I was told that I wasn't wanted for the present. Miss Rampick had collapsed from severe exhaustion. All thoughts of questioning her would have to be deferred. I tried to convey to them that finding Rampick was a matter of some urgency because the man was not capable of looking after himself.

I half expected to find Brenda waiting for me on my return, intrigued by the arrival of the police car and ambulance. She still had a key to my flat. It was unusually quiet as I approached Ruskin House. The only person in the hot dusty forecourt was a boy who two or three years earlier used to enrage me by his dumb insolence. He used to play with a gang of hooligans who spent their time writing on the staircase walls, and fighting, bellowing and making metallic music with sticks and bicycle pumps on the banisters. In my mind the boy was associated with Brenda's adultery because that particular nuisance belonged to the time when I first suspected her of being unfaithful to me. Whenever I shouted at the children and broke up a game of cops and robbers the same boy would remain unimpressed by my shouts, standing erect with his back to the wall or even perfectly still in the doorway like a statue in its niche, a sly smile playing about the corners of his mouth. Eventually I came to the conclusion that this was more than just a case of youthful defiance. Didn't his smile signify that he despised me and my theatrical fury because he knew for certain what I was merely beginning to suspect? Now, with the same restrained mockery, he watched me approach the big metal doors. His evident interest in my movements gave me the idea that he knew someone was waiting for me but I passed no one on the stairs.

CHAPTER THIRTEEN

I unlocked the door of my flat and paused. No smell of cigarettes. No histrionic cough. (Brenda alone). No suppressed giggle (Brenda and friend). I closed the front-door gently and tiptoed down the passage to the living-room.

Rampick was sitting in the armchair, his black 'adidas' bag at his feet.

He glanced up at me then looked away. I noticed his hands were trembling. I sat down before I spoke, the key still in my hand. The key prompted me to ask the obvious question.

I could tell by his expression that he no longer, figuratively speaking, wore the prisoner's mask. His first words to me as a contemporary were about the door being unlocked.

I detected a slight difference in his voice. In tone. In register. It was as subtly altered as his facial expression and was much more like his sister's voice and accent.

'You must have left in a hurry,' he said.

What he said was perfectly true. In the haste and confusion of leaving I couldn't remember closing the door.

'Where is Sylvia?' he asked.

I told him what had happened. Rampick explained that he had been lying low until Sylvia told him it was safe to come out.

'Where were you?' I asked.

He smiled. 'Where else but in the great sea-facing bastion strengthened by Vauban.'

He added, to explain how he had got inside, 'hooligans have forced an entry.'

It seemed that the arrival of unwelcome company had extended his stay there. But for the embarrassment of revealing his presence, he would have ventured out much earlier whether Sylvia had returned or not. I guessed at once, largely by his facial expression as he pronounced the words 'unwelcome company', that he meant that the gross and dwarfish Ursula had brought a client there.

The thought of Rampick watching her perform in her professional capacity took me back to the first months of abstinence after Brenda had left me. The existence of a woman like that living in the same building had been a disturbing influence. This was some months before I became engrossed in the legend of the Man in the Iron Mask and the clinical (or rather, as now appeared more likely, dramaturgic) history of Rampick.

With a mocking inflexion, but otherwise speaking in the voice I was accustomed to, Rampick seemed to confirm the accuracy of my intuition by murmuring softly, 'The whore from the Tuileries.'

Increasingly, as I studied him, I noticed that this was a rejuvenated Rampick — cleaner shaven and generally rather smarter in appearance. His old raincoat was the opposite of a *cache-misère* concealing shabbiness, since beneath the un-buttoned coat the sports jacket he was wearing looked new. Once I thought I glimpsed the steel bracelet of a watch on his wrist. Perhaps I was mistaken. Or perhaps the watch was pushed so far up his skeletal forearm that it was only rarely visible.

I asked him directly if I was correct in assuming he had been play-acting all the time. Rampick was inclined to quibble over terminology. What precisely did I mean by 'play-acting'? There had been nothing frivolous, he assured me, about the time he had spent on research or the efforts he had made to give to each of our encounters a theme and a structure. Did I appreciate the constant alertness that was needed to recognize and seize every opportunity to exploit the fortuitous word, the smallest incident, the slightest noise from outside? And all the time also he was striving unobtrusively to draw the best out of me.

'You have a rare capacity for suspending disbelief,' he in-formed me 'But few natural talents as an actor.'

'Anyway,' he continued, 'that was not so important, and your performance improved remarkably once I had decided on a role for you. Neither the role of Aramis nor the role of d'Artagnan suited your personality at all. You are not mercurial. You are not imperious. You are not masterful and boastful. You are not filled with Jesuitical cunning. You are, in fact, Saint-Mars. To a T — reliable, diligent, honourable, taciturn.'

He hoped that I would not be so short-sighted as to dismiss the seriousness of his point of view now that I realized his performance had been rationally conceived and executed. He had taken infinite pains to vary his approach in order to sustain my interest. He had been particularly gratified when I had discovered quite independently *The Memoirs of d'Artagnan*. The greater the knowledge I acquired, the more satisfying our level of discourse.

Obviously his own resources were not boundless. His guiding principles had been to remain consistent without becoming monotonous, to simulate the madman's cunning extempore but never extravagantly. If his chief progenitor had been the King of Lies, he hoped the Muses (of History and Tragedy) had also been involved.

'And surely,' he said, 'you don't imagine I would expend all that effort for no better reason than to sneer at you when your back was turned. I deceived you only to sustain the illusion.'

'It is a pity that I accumulated a good deal of material I won't be able to use. I had a small gallery of characters I was going to introduce. My efforts were unscripted, by and large, and some of my happiest touches were improvisations. Still, planning is always essential. . . . The Mancini sisters, long past their prime, I was going to introduce. Also the scoundrelly Lauzun. And the Scottish prisoner Seldon who was released when King Louis was briefly incarcerated in my stead. There is no point in regretting now the pleasure I might have had.

'But I must take this opportunity to thank you for the necessary part you played and for your appreciation. All my previous partners in rudimentary, unsatisfactory charades were marplots — simply too impatient to spend time on the finer details of the plot.'

'I see,' I said. 'And your sister . . .'

'It is unfortunate,' he interrupted, 'that Sylvia panicked over my interest in that young thug. But Sylvia, you know, cannot reconcile herself to the infirmities of the flesh. Her aloofness from the physical makes her regard lovemaking of any kind as grotesque. . . . There was never any doubt that I would get the credit for the attack on that depraved boy. I could imagine, I could hear your voice, earnestly explaining that the poor lunatic, enmeshed in his historical fantasies, would think he was defending himself against a hired assassin. . . .

'Perhaps my ugly little sister will confess. And supposing she does, will they believe her? After the years she has spent as a slave to duty protecting and excusing me? Does it seem likely?'

Rampick's voice was steady yet his hands never stopped moving. Half-smiles and frowns alternated with bewildering rapidity. There was also an eager almost predatory look that I hadn't observed in the past.

'Would you mind saying something as the Man in the Iron Mask?' I asked him.

'I can't think of anything,' he sniggered. 'I'm not in the mood. . . . Wait a moment, though!'

He cleared his throat.

'*Let us go where the crown of France is to be found! . . . Shall I never cease to hearken to the scruples of my heart?*'

His face was briefly the familiar face I knew. The lines he quoted were thrown away ironically but the voice was recognizable again.

Reverting to his unfamiliar 'normal' voice he said: 'I have always been highly critical of Dumas. Wouldn't you agree with me that his scenes and situations are seldom even half way realized? The most pictorial and picturesque aspects of his romances are never fully exploited.

'Still that left me plenty of scope to develop on the original. . . . The Man in the Iron Mask is my favourite role and at least for short periods I escaped from the abominable present day.'

Rampick gestured towards the window.

'The ignoble chaos out there. That was the attraction for you wasn't it? To imagine it was somehow possible to abolish *that*. To get rid of it and still remain sentient, though stark mad, your head teeming with inventions all your own, enjoying a *"secret prodigality of being"*, the inner resources that don't exist for normal adult people, the kind that spend their leisure time banging and hammering. I did, in fact, do my utmost to push myself to the frontiers of paranoia. It was your faith in my sincerity that spurred me on. Your amazing faith! Such a profound disciple!'

Had his attempt at suicide been play-acting too? I repeated the word 'play-acting' deliberately to provoke him.

'Suicide was only your assumption, and it was a false assumption,' Rampick told me.

That ill-starred day, for some trivial misdemeanour, Sylvia had locked him in his room with her favourite Max. On impulse in a fury he had hurled the struggling snapping lap-dog out of the back window. Unfortunately, in his zeal to dispose of the creature, he had leaned too far out himself.

Ignoring my dismay at this disclosure (horror mingled with some incredulity), Rampick turned to his sister's eager connivance in my deception. From the first she had encouraged it, or at least as soon as she realized it was essentially different from previous charades that had added a touch of fantasy to sexual encounters.

'It was her favourite illusion to think of me as a harmless lunatic instead of a filthy pederast. She looked on my relationship with you as the finest "ideal" friendship of my life. But it was to end quite soon. Quite soon I was scheduled to recover my wits.'

He paused.

'Sylvia, in her innocence, didn't foresee how dull a friendship ours would be without the spice of fantasy!'

His smile was so impertinent that I must have made an involuntary aggressive movement. He exchanged the impertinent smile for a dubiously authentic look of alarm.

'The Girl Guide approved of you because your interest in me was not sexual. Apparently not. Humanitarian? Or was it art for art's sake? We discussed this from time to time. It was difficult to decide to what extent you had convinced yourself you were humouring a poor madman and to what extent you had become unbalanced by the contagion of a counterfeit insanity.'

'Sylvia thought you were good for me. The right sort of caring, "straight" friend for my middle years. But at times she feared for your sanity, especially when you spoke to her of dreams that were so vivid that even afterwards you could not accept them as merely dreams. Dreams within dreams you spoke of. Awakenings that were the disguised continuations of dreams. I would have liked to hear you describe these dreams my "madness" had inspired. They were very drily and briefly relayed to me. Sylvia saw that you were so drawn towards a life of fantasy that your own hold on reason might grow precarious.'

Without any transition (and no sign of embarrassment that I could distinguish from his general restlessness) Rampick changed the subject to his pressing need for money. It would be best both for him and for his sister (taking the long view) if they could achieve a final irrevocable break. For this he needed a loan to take him right away from the area. He had tried before now, unsuccessfully, to spare his sister further years of senseless protracted guardianship. Her unappreciated lavishing on him of unwholesome sisterly devotion! She had forgiven him too much — her own wasted years of service, his ingratitude, the sadistic tricks he had played on her. Even the 'defenestration of Max' had not destroyed her sense of obligation to take care of him. This new cynical and heartless Rampick (an individual I could not at all identify with the former gentle recluse of that name) seemed in high spirits at the prospect of a life of freedom that previously I had thought would have been anathema to him, believing his only desire to be shut away permanently in his solitary grandeur.

'Surely you could have escaped from your sister's guardianship long ago if you'd really wanted to,' I suggested.

My assumption of Rampick's life-long financial dependence on his sister was confirmed by what he said next.

'It is true,' he conceded, 'that I have always found working and living incompatible, my natural sluggishness at odds with my desire for independence.'

I told him it seemed (to say the least) unlikely that he would be able to support himself by impersonating the masked prisoner of the Bastille, adding in an attempt to upset his intolerable self-possession, that according to Dr Scullard his literary efforts were not original.

Rampick made no comment on this. He merely said he could understand my bitterness. For his part he was sorry our collaboration had come to an end. An audience of one where the one was as appreciative and involved as I had been was all the audience he desired. But he could see that from my viewpoint the disappointment must be equally great. Perhaps greater. I must feel I had been cheated out of a profound relationship with an exceptional creature who appeared to have access to modes of being unknown to rational man, a state of affairs that had perhaps been a little frightening at times but was also fascinating.

'Believe me!' Rampick said, 'I understand your chagrin. In your place I would feel mortified, disappointed, perhaps even vengeful. And you must feel it is a poor sort of exchange to have lost a kingly shadow . . . and gained . . .'

His voice faltered and died on 'substance' as he watched me cross the room to the phone. He waited until I had finished dialling before he began his unobtrusive departure. I listened for the front door to close, as it did quite gently. I replaced the receiver without having uttered a word.

There was no reviving a ghost. The kingly shadow, the King of Murk-Light had gone. A figment. Meanwhile the substance, the trickster, masker, counterfeit madman, specialist in mummery, in metachronism, was making his exit from Ruskin House. The heavy metal doors slammed behind him.

I counted up to ten.

Rampick was nowhere in sight in the sunny forecourt of the flats. No children. No adults. No dogs even. Brenda's washing — shirts, towels, sheets — motionless in the far corner.

I walked back through the swing doors and out at the back. Ursula was in her kitchen. Day-dreaming at the sink. Her skirt rucked up, she absently scratched her thigh, painted fingernails delved for the elusive scab-mite.

I had almost made a circuit of the mill before I came to the nailed boards that hooligans had ripped down. No one seemed to be watching as I ducked in through a narrow opening. Rampick, waiting just inside, took my arm. The ground was uneven. Before my eyes grew accustomed to the dimness I stumbled over a coiled mass of rusty chains.

Rampick said nothing about my supposed summoning of the police.

'It was hereabouts, in this corner, that the couple I told you about were so preoccupied.'

'I'm surprised at your interest,' I said.

'*You* would have been *more* interested,' he replied. 'You were quick to assume I was referring to that bloated turnip-faced blonde whose premises act as a magnet to middle-aged suburban husbands. Their eyes bigger than their appetites. Their appetites bigger than their capacities.'

'Who was it, then?' I asked.

'A vivacious brunette. Well known to you. And a handsome, passionate Italian. Well, passionate at least. The ice-cream vendor. Ah! *Bellissima! Carissima!* . . . I am not suggesting your wife takes money for that sort of thing. They must have succumbed to an urgent need. I wasn't the only spectator. At one time that fat boy with the sly look was peering in from outside. I can't imagine he would see very much from out there.'

Rampick had moved to another corner of the room, the first room of many rooms perhaps. It was darker in this corner. There were smashed up crates and the rusty remains of machinery. Gory dew on the walls. A smell of damp and excreta.

'There is a dead dog over there,' whispered Rampick. 'Under a sack. The stench is appalling if you go within yards of it.'

'Talking of voyeurism,' he said. 'When I lived in the flats (and by the way I never thought that one day I would see the inside of this ruin) you seemed happy to watch me, as I sat pen in hand, gazing at that great blind wall with the advertisement for hats. Don't you think that was a kind of voyeurism? Watching the madman deep in his private illusions?'

'Actually,' Rampick continued, 'your visits were becoming

too regular. I was getting stale. I was running short of ideas. Finally I was compelled to write to Sylvia to come and take me away from here. Also I was in need of money at the time. . . . However, as soon as I was back home my interest in our little drama flared up again and I soon grew tired of the continual proximity of my sister. . . . After my accident we both thought that a visit from you every fortnight or so would be about right. It would give Sylvia some company too. She probably also dreamed of wedding bells, chiefly I think with my interests at heart. She was working on you to drop the formality of "Miss Rampick". I told her (cruelly I'm afraid) that on the days she didn't smell of furniture polish she smelled of camphor and always wore the same wide, brown, pleated corduroy skirt that resembled the covering for a table in some old cottage lit by an oil lamp. . . . As for myself I was planning a series of virtuoso performances, spectacular climaxes, and then quite a sudden recovery (all good things must come to an end) until that boy started prowling about and unsettled me.'

I touched him on the shoulder and said: '*Let us go where the crown of France is to be found!*'

He gave an incredulous laugh and resisted the pressure.

'Seriously,' I said. 'Shall we explore the rest of your starfort?'

I withdrew from my pocket the paper-knife I had armed myself with before leaving the flat. Slender and nearly a foot long it was a formidable weapon. With a short, alarmed laugh, Rampick moved ahead of me through an opening.

CHAPTER FOURTEEN

Rampick was too wary of my knife to say what he was thinking as I compelled him to go upstairs. Chinks of daylight were distasteful reminders to me of the continuing existence of the bedlamite world outside. (That world of alien presences, in particular alien sounds, mechanical, human, animal — the animal were the least insupportable, motorbikes and football cannonades were the most prolonged, but the worst, the least predictable, the most scarifying, were the human noises, and the worst of these were the unexpected female screams, the operatic blood-curdling screams, at dusk or in the middle of the night, the virtuoso performances of depraved schoolgirls, blatantly not cries for help but encouragement of 'unwelcome' attentions, inciting further outrage, greater violation . . .).

As we climbed the stairs it grew darker. Rampick was commendably silent. At the outset he had clearly doubted my resolution, contemptuous because he had been able to deceive me for so long. To teach him greater respect I had lunged at his tattered mackintosh with the mother-of-pearl-handled knife. But even under duress Rampick showed quite remarkable composure. Clearly his was too proud a nature to stoop and cringe. (He lacked, that is to say, my own menial and cowardly instincts.) Nevertheless he was not so proud as to defy me altogether and encourage me to commit murder in the second degree. When he stumbled, when he expressed doubts about the safety of the stairs, I told him I was 'shit sick of his puling talk', adding that first gross and unnecessary epithet much against my normal habits of speech. And this outburst was a piece of blatant exaggeration on my part because, to be fair to this mincing *roitelet*, he had spoken quite coolly about the dangers of the old building. In fact a certain trepidation in the circumstances was only natural and reasonable.

He didn't speak again until we reached a bright dusty glass-strewn workroom with a skylight at either end that had been painted over navy blue. It was hot beneath the darkened skylights after a day of sun.

At the far end there was a small section of dusty skylight neither painted blue nor smashed. Here we were presented with a minor miracle of appositeness. I responded to it with eagerness. By contrast Rampick's enthusiasm left a great deal to be desired. Was this because of the knife I brandished? Was it because, in the past, the enjoyment of practising a deception had been more crucial than he had been prepared to admit? With the narrow blade a hair's breadth from his pullet neck I compelled Rampick to look upwards. It seemed incredible that here I was needing to coerce him into sharing my appreciation of the conceit that in this old mill, once part of his island fortress of Sainte Marguerite, we were reunited with a sort of kingly shadow. A black and dusty regal silhouette. Rampick gazed up but only at my prompting. He ventured no comment and his face, I was disappointed to see, revealed no genuine interest. I, on the contrary, was all but overwhelmed by the spectacle. I only regret that in describing it now I will communicate nothing of the feelings, the abundance of warm excited feelings that filled me almost to overflowing, feelings of superstitious awe, feelings that were almost sensual, feelings that coexisted so strangely, so irksomely, with personal vexation at the provocative lukewarmness of my companion. I could scarcely endure it that this Frenchless unexalted *diseur*, this counterfeit princeling neither distinguished by royal blood nor by madness, after imposing his far-fetched fictions on me, now had the gall to exhibit virtual indifference in the face of such an astonishingly appropriate emblem. On the skylight in one corner, the shadow of a bishop chimney-pot was cast aslant on the dusty panes. The square brickwork of the chimney-shaft was transformed by the oblique angle into convincing sloping humanoid shoulders. The long evening shadows converted the chimney-pot itself into an elongated visored crowned head with an almost horizontal slightly downwards curving slit (the occularium) visible a convincing two-thirds the way up the great helm.

Rampick looked at his watch. He did have a watch, I noted.

It was twenty-past six. I put down the knife; to be precise I stood it erect in the crevice between two floor-boards. Already I had had my fill of the paltry satisfactions of terrorism in which you end up chiefly frightening yourself. I fancied that a number of crates and two rickety chairs were arranged in a semi-circle in front of a non-existent blackboard or dais or lectern.

'We have plenty of time to talk,' I said to Rampick. 'Please be seated!'

I indicated the rickety-looking chairs that had slug tracks across the damp and shiny seats. Rampick muttered and remained standing.

I proceeded to lecture him on the subject of Alexandre Dumas. 'Like coals to Newcastle,' I openly admitted. And by the way, I added, 'Is it not curious that whenever the musketeers came musketeering to this country they invariably turned up in Newcastle?'

My spontaneous lecture was entirely suggested by the arrangement of chairs and crates. I warmed to my theme.

'Dumas is a hasty slipshod author best read at a gallop,' I began.

In my mind was an image of page after page printed as a deterrent to appreciation in an awful, intensely black and vulgar type-face like miles and miles of iron railings.

'The nineteenth century,' I continued, 'paid scant attention to Dumas' literary shortcomings. Even the most stylistically-sensitive (George Saintsbury for example) responded enthusiastically to "something" in the great romancer — whether to the amiability and simple-heartedness of the implied author, the pace of the narrative, the bold characterization, even (and this would be strangest of all) to the climactic grandiose sentimental-epic or operatic effects.'

Rampick seemed to be listening — with interest or not it was impossible to tell.

'By contrast, we of the twentieth century see little in Dumas except his remoteness from reality, his stageyness, and an undistinguished style that veers from the careless and plain to the meretricious, with the occasional exceptional set piece that reads like the apprentice work of an enthusiastic schoolboy showing his admiration (through pastiche) for Hugo or Châteaubriand.

'But this is all preamble. It is of no significance at all.'

I noticed that Rampick was nowhere to be seen, which was small wonder and hardly worth thinking about either.

'It seems to me that one of the crucial and universally ignored aspects of literary appreciation is how much and what exactly it is, what the residue is, left from a reading, one year, two years, three years, and much longer afterwards. And the fact that when the reader returns to a book, perhaps a decade, perhaps two decades later, the one visual image, the one episode of any particular significance to that reader . . . is nowhere to be found in the text however thorough the re-reading. The incident of Athos convalescent in the bedroom of the inn and the assassin creeping in by the casement may be one such incident. In fact I am convinced that the talented artist who executed that illustration was genuinely deceived by the after-image of just some such phantom episode, a distorting trick of memory.'

I waited as though for applause or questions or to enable the stifled cough to be released like a ragged volley of musketry. I was looking towards the kingly shadow that was rather less sharply etched than before. Then I noticed Rampick again. He was creeping up behind me as though playing at grandmother's steps. He had prised up my discarded dagger from the floor. It was in his left hand — no doubt for safe keeping so that I couldn't threaten mischief with it. In his other hand he held an iron bar. Obviously his new role was that of keeper. We had changed places. Now it was a question of Rampick humouring me — or rather, as humouring did not appear to be his style, intimidating, disciplining me. I could hardly blame him for taking the opportunity to arm himself. He could not have known that I had had no serious intention of ever using that stiletto for any other purpose than to slit open envelopes. At the same time, as though I were intoxicated, I was overflowing again with inappropriate, inspired, puissant and expansive feelings; the searing pain of the blade entering my arm was, in a sense, a climax of these feelings, ecstasy and agony combined, although the agony almost immediately dispersed the bewitching aura and the blow of the iron bar was a merciful release.

My powers of expression are not equal to conveying intensity of pain. I speak as if from hearsay. If I were to speak now, belatedly, on oath, in the court-room, I would speak of that day as I have written of it. Not the whole truth but as much of the truth as I remember.

I imagine Rampick's 'truth' would be rather different.

CHAPTER FIFTEEN

And so it proved; but Rampick's version of the events of that day was not accepted and it was a long time before I was in a position to give any kind of a coherent version of my own, either to corroborate or to contradict his. Only gradually did the substance of what had taken place return to me.

Sylvia Rampick's confession that it had been she who had struck the youth was not accepted either. Her attempts to blacken my character by arguing that I was the chief culprit, instigator, corrupting influence, greater madman, greater danger to the public, met with no success. After all I was not implicated in the attack on the youth. And Miss Rampick could scarcely maintain that the knife wound in my shoulder and the more serious head injuries were self-inflicted.

The doctors told me that I was making a tolerably good recovery. With luck I should continue to improve steadily over the coming months. I had lost my sense of taste and smell — temporarily. My vision was slightly affected but was likely to improve. Some other symptoms (migraine, dizziness, *echo de la pensée*) I had had previously but I kept this information to myself. Whatever else followed from the blow to my skull, I was determined to reap the benefit of subsidized idleness.

I have said that my sight and my sense of taste and smell were affected. But far more significant than these was the effect on my hearing. This condition, the doctors assured me, was also unlikely to be permanent. However, for the present, the volume of sound from outside was very much reduced. Quite regularly, if I happened to look out of my window, I was taken aback at the sight of children playing on the threadbare grass. A moment earlier I had been completely unaware of their existence. Usually I didn't hear my doorbell. Very rarely did I know that the postman had delivered a letter. (This was not exactly a major catastrophe since the postman, as far as I am concerned, has never been anything but a walking disappointment.)

After leaving hospital I was nursed by Brenda. There was no question of a reconciliation between us; in fact she had begun to talk about a divorce again. I didn't mention the Italian and Rampick's Peeping Tom story. Perhaps it was true, there was nothing inherently implausible in it. At the same time I had come to the conclusion that Rampick took pleasure in repudiating truth on principle. Lying for lying's sake.

My relationship with Brenda was amicable enough, but as soon as I was able to get about and manage more or less everything myself she came less frequently and stayed very briefly, as though embarrassed or guilty at being with me at all.

Rampick was committed, for his own good, for the two crimes of violence — only one of which can I be certain he was guilty of. And there were extenuating circumstances surrounding his attack on me that were not brought out. My peculiar mental state that evening, my provocative behaviour with the knife, I had never described precisely, honestly, and fully. At first I genuinely could not remember all the details. A truthful comprehensive account (such as I have written here, I believe, and such as Rampick's testimony in many respects corroborated) was at that time utterly beyond my capacity.

The few odd revelations that I had divulged, evidence of Rampick's sadistic impulses (the killing of his sister's dog and the black cat) naturally did him no good at all, and I was convinced that my part in her brother's committal had earned me Miss Rampick's undying hatred. She was a sinister figure to me now. La Voisin in earnest. I seriously thought she might take steps to avenge her brother, especially if Rampick's claim that it had been she who struck the youth was true. I was in two minds whether to believe him.

I was therefore expecting and dreading a visit from Miss Rampick. Instead I had a visit from an acquaintance, almost a stranger to me. Telling him the history of my injuries and rather inarticulately sketching in the background made me realize fully what a dubious, peculiar business it was.

I was embarrassed talking to him. I didn't succeed in finding a suitable tone. And my nervousness was increased by the man's stern, unsympathetic attitude, his tense posture, his hostile eyes. I was unable to comprehend the motive for his visit until he revealed, as he was on the point of leaving, that he knew the Rampicks well; it seemed they were half-cousins of his. And I was mortified and astounded by his final words, to which he gave a definitive jeering emphasis, that the Philip Rampick he had known from childhood wouldn't hurt a fly.

It had been sultry all day and as this visitor walked away from the flats the first peals of thunder sounded, descending (within a couple of seconds) from piercing falsetto to sniggering bass, and then, after a brief pause, culminating in a dull explosion. Since even I heard it distinctly, the noise to normal ears must have been tremendous. I watched my visitor from the window. He never faltered in his stride. By contrast, at the final detonation several other people, including two elderly women, a window-cleaner carrying his bucket and ladder, and the Italian Mauvilli, who happened to be outside just then, all jumped noticeably at the same moment — the old women in unison clapped a hand to their bosoms, and from nowhere a fawn lurcher shot across the forecourt and out of sight round a corner. I stepped back myself as the window rattled.

The same afternoon, through my usually constipated letter-box, slipped a letter from Miss Rampick. I found it in the passage some distance from the front door. As there was no stamp on the envelope (and it was long past second post) it must have been delivered by hand. By Miss Rampick herself? The thought of her lurking close by filled me with unease and precipitated a coward's recklessness. Straight away, leaving the door ajar, in my carpet slippers and oldest clothes, I rushed out on to the landing. I checked the meter cupboard next to the dust chute. I went up to the next landing. I descended to the basement. Walking briskly, even running a few steps, I started off round the block. Before long I felt sick and dizzy and was forced to abandon the futile chase. From her kitchen the harlot looked at me as I passed. She actually looked at me, a gleam of recognition in her eyes, perhaps even a look of sympathy. I tried to recollect her name. My difficulty over names was probably a result of my injuries. Back in my flat I checked all the rooms. I opened the wardrobe. I looked under the beds. When a shadow fell across the opaque glass square in the front door, my heart began to pound. However, a moment later, I was reassured by the familiar loud wheezing that always announced the return from work of the stout, garrulous, indomitable old woman who lived across the landing. . . .

The envelope was damp. Did this mean that it had been delivered during the cloudburst that had followed my hostile visitor's departure and the first peal of thunder? Then it occurred to me as strange that if Miss Rampick had delivered the letter, the envelope should have been exposed to the rain and not kept in her handbag.

As I tore open the envelope an image came to mind. Another fragment returning from my last confrontation with her brother. The image was trivial enough; an image of Rampick struggling to see the time by the watch pushed far up his scrawny forearm. But that was enough, together with the sight of his sister's handwriting, to bring the man's presence, the way he looked, the way he held himself, almost palpably into the room.

I had anticipated the general tenor and some of the contents of Miss Rampick's letter — the terrible state of mind Rampick was in at the asylum (the authorities quickly lose patience with a defiant lunatic but her brother knew he was no lunatic) — the disgraceful treacherous part I had played in his committal — the friendship that had been extended to me, the trust reposed in me — the unforgivable way I had repaid their friendship and their trust. No mention of Rampick's deceitful masquerade. No mention of the knife wound, the blow from the iron bar. It could not be construed as a threatening letter, however. And neither was I being urged to any course of action. No appeal, for example to my conscience to help her secure Rampick's release. There was one jibe at my sanity. An ironic allusion to my enthusiasm for the kingly silhouette. Rampick must have described this to her. The words 'a sane man's natural reverence for a baked fireclay monarch' were almost certainly Rampick's own. All in all the letter could have been much more unpleasant. I put it on one side feeling somewhat relieved.

Perhaps as a reaction (or perhaps because of my general condition) I immediately fell asleep in my armchair.

I was not to feel reassured for long. Some hours later I noticed a glimmer of white in the dark hallway. When I switched the light on I saw the familiar pictures of the wounded musketeer and his would-be assassin affixed to my wall in the same place they had occupied in the flat upstairs. (Looking exactly the same because the background, the chipboard paper, is the same in all the entrance passages.) The lower of the two pictures was not quite straight. There was no question of sleep that night. At regular intervals I felt compelled to pace from room to room, looking behind the doors, in the wardrobe, in the airing-cupboard, under beds. In particular, with increasing frequency, I checked and rechecked the front-door catch. At one time I sobbed or rather whimpered (stifling my sobs) because there was no bar I could slide on for extra security.

I didn't sleep the next night either. Far too early I drank the remains of my whisky so that I was sober again at the worst time, in the early hours. The following afternoon, despite my tiredness, I escaped from the flats for a walk in the suburbs.

Although I came back most of the way on a bus, I was so exhausted that my sense of my own identity had begun to flicker and dwindle alarmingly until finally my self-awareness seemed detached, receding from my body. In the flat as soon as I sat down I lost consciousness. I assume I fainted from weakness. I dreamed (at least just before I woke I was dreaming) of an ancient musketeer with a walrus moustache, the face of Flaubert or Oliver Hardy, who was posing on the lower steps of an immense staircase. While one gauntleted hand rested on the banister, with the other the musketeer caressed the triumphant embonpoint that swelled out his dark blue *casaque* in a manner ludicrously recalling that of a nine-month pregnant woman fondling (with immense serene satisfaction) the maternity smock draped over the almost ripe fruit in her womb. . . .

The telephone woke me. It was Brenda. She told me she had called round and had got no answer. I explained that a walk had tired me. I must have been asleep. I was in two minds whether to tell her I suspected Rampick's sister of playing tricks to make me doubt my sanity. But Brenda, sunny and vivacious as ever, had rung off before I decided to broach the subject.

The telephone is on the window-sill. As I looked up I thought I saw Miss Rampick disappearing round the corner of the flats opposite. I told myself the distance had been too great for me to be sure it was her. I tried to convince myself by recalling other instances of mistaken perception, such as when an old woman trudging has become, at a closer view, a young woman in evident torment from uncomfortable boots or shoes. Nothing however satisfied me that I had been mistaken. I was left with no alternative. To overcome my fears, to disperse the uncanny atmosphere I was helping to create, I would have to take the initiative and confront Sylvia Rampick at her home. This resolution taken I managed to sleep fitfully.

CHAPTER SIXTEEN

The superstitious dread I had felt the previous nights had evaporated. Now that their lines of circumvallation had been drawn, it was plain that my own hope of salvation lay in a surprise counter-attack. I must take the offensive. I must seek out my shadowy adversaries, even though I had little chance, in my present weakened state, against the concerted efforts of that rancorous pair, exalted as they must be by the joy of intrigue and the joyful prospect of a soon-to-be consummated vengeance.

My sole comfort lay in the knowledge that only one of my enemies could manoeuvre freely. (Unless there were others, hired reformadoes, that I had no information about.) Nevertheless I was under no illusion that Miss Rampick alone would prove anything less than a formidable antagonist — her brother's able and willing regent, lieutenant, seasoned campaigner, reliable, skilled and experienced in her traditional role as intermediary, courier and spy, a relentless, homely-featured Miladi to Rampick's villainous Rochefort. Above all I must be careful not to underestimate the woman's natural shrewdness.

Still less to be underestimated or overlooked was Rampick himself. Darkly motionless in the background but at the heart of the web, Rampick would see himself in the no doubt congenial role of arch-conspirator. As the Man of Meung perhaps. As the great cardinal even. Behind the scenes Rampick would direct operations. He would exercise to the utmost all his resources, all his ingenuity to bring about my disgrace, my ultimate ruin, with the 'justifiable' aim (justifiable, that is, in the mind of that perverse philanthropist) that I might be reclaimed, might be persuaded to renounce my apostasy, and one day be reunited with him in his secret citadel.

It seemed as though henceforward, schooled by Rampick, I

might only be capable of thinking positively in this unrealistic, uncontemporary, bombastic, war-gaming fashion. If I were to think of the Rampicks in a more appropriate manner as an ageing pair of malicious, spiteful and peculiar individuals, immediately I had insufficient strength to fight them. And in that case my only future would be a defensive, beleaguered, unbearable one, a life of persecution and continual strain.

I was in a state of feverish excitement, the impatience of a weak man desperate to act precipitately, when I arrived at Blackhorse Terrace.

I rang the doorbell. No one answered. Through a narrow gap between lace curtains I peered into the dark front room. The vertical sliver of glass contained a bewildering variety of reflected phenomena. Bright-edged, black-centred clouds and chimneys, dormer windows, TV aerials, all hindered direct unreflected vision, so that I was almost prevented from establishing that the sofa, the upright piano, the low glass-fronted bookcase cum china cupboard and everything else that I less clearly remembered had been removed.

The estate agent's sign in the garden (partly masked by the diagonal red-on-white paper baldrick SOLD) should have alerted me to the possibility that the house might be empty, the unbeautiful chatelaine departed. Far too easily I had allowed myself to be deceived by the curtains that still hung at all the windows.

Yet I rang the bell again. I knocked again. A dozen times at least I knocked. Later, at the estate agents, I was refused a forwarding address. They had been given precise instructions not to give any inquirer whatever, not excepting close friends and relations, the present address of the former occupiers. They seemed unwilling even to mention the Rampicks by name. New people should have moved into the property by this time but there had been some delay. Estate agent and receptionist vied with each other to practise their firmest resolve, their most discouraging manner on me. Suitably chastened I turned and walked self-consciously to the door. I winced as I caught the doorstep with my shoulder, the same shoulder that had been pierced with a stiletto as I lay convalescing in the country inn.

For an undefined length of time I was in a state of utter confusion. Not until I reached the familiar district between the railway-station and Blackhorse Terrace did I begin to recover my wits and become aware of my surroundings. For some reason also there was a blank where the recollection of the morning train journey ought to have been. To get from point A to point B clearly presupposes a journey of some kind. (Unless it was all a dream.) I thought back to the straightforward early days when I had humoured the *ci-devant* royal twin. A pathological episode. A *folie à deux*. But naive and honest on my part. Then, it transpired, it was play-acting. It had been play-acting all the time. Then, with another turn of the wheel, it became a pathological episode once more with Rampick the pervert, the unconventional mummer, certified, put in confinement, while my own temporary lapse, derangement you may call it, went unpunished. (Unconfessed. Uncorroborated.) Now again it was play-acting. Cruder this time. Less genial. Play-acting with a purpose since the dead tree's sylvan sister (denuded of blossom or greenery, the human counterpart of a withered, storm-blasted old blackthorn) was acting under instructions (there could be no doubt about this) to work me up to such a pitch of insanity that I would conclude by begging for admittance at the lodge gates of the private drive (I pictured it a *cottage orné* of a lodge, a notice, STRICTLY NO ADMITTANCE, a drive twisting through dense shrubberies) to the madhouse, the poet Mahalin's *Maison de Santé*. . . . A pathological episode also, with sinister implications for me.

I approached the house once more. This time the door opened. As I started to ascend the *escalier derobé* the uncarpeted steps creaked. A familiar though rather muffled voice invited me to come straight up. A command rather than an invitation. I obeyed with alacrity. Then a shiver of dread made me stop so abruptly that I stumbled, I hugged the steps; the topmost of them bruised my chin as I fell.

What awaited me in the prisoner's cell? I was unarmed, unprotected. Appalled at my recklessness I remained cowering on the stairs.

' "Never pat a dog on the head when he is expecting food!" is sound advice, Saint-Mars. If you have no positive news to give me, it is best that you restrict your comments to the bare essentials.'

I looked up. The prisoner was standing above me on the landing. Apparently he saw nothing incongruous, nothing improper in conversing thus with his gaoler who was sprawled so ignominiously at his feet.

The prisoner's voice from within the great helmet was muffled and metallic.

'Of course when I die,' the helmeted figure mused aloud, 'they will say I was poisoned just like any other great personage.'

'This evening,' he resumed, with a disregard of natural transitions and a quotidian inaccuracy entirely typical of him: 'Before you came, I was thinking of the career of the cold, ambitious, imperious Bishop of Vannes. You will remember that he betrayed me and all his own plans, inadvertently, by divulging the secret of the imposture to his theoretically obvious ally, the unexpectedly loyal and honourable Surintendant Fouquet. The ground had already been undermined beneath me while I played my futile role bravely at my first and last *petite levée* in the face of the Queen Mother's ill-disguised perplexity. It was obvious that she would never accept the strange alteration in her proud son's mannerisms, in the timbre of his voice. But how did Aramis come to make such a terrible blunder? Just imagine! To reveal the secret so directly! With such a lapse to his credit how could that musketeer in a cassock ever hope to regain his credibility as the epitome of Jesuitical cunning and hold on to his exalted position as General of the Order? Belle Isle was not sure enough, not remote enough to bury his shame. Neither 'impregnable' Belle Isle nor Kimpercorentin nor Spain were remote enough. Even New France was not sufficiently far removed to bury the shame of that disgraced caballer.

'You may rise now, Saint-Mars! I accept your abject apology. You provoked me intolerably. I was in a frenzy the night I struck you. An act unworthy even of my brother. It was inhuman of me to overlook the fact that all mankind is not equipped with a steel-reinforced cranium. Your poor unprotected skull cracked like an egg as I brought down my stick. Your undoing was your provoking symbololatry. While you venerated the shadow of kingship, the wronged man took his opportunity to wreak a belated vengeance on his oppressors in the person of his loyal friend and considerate gaoler. Yet one more example, I am afraid, of the injustice of life and literature and legend.

'And now, Saint-Mars, it is imperative that we go in search of some new locutory! Some new reclusory! It is impossible to talk freely in such a public place.'

According to Dostoevsky's 'raw youth' there is always a moment when a drunken man is aware that he is intoxicated and at that moment he is entirely sober. Such a moment arrived for me when I realized I was living through a series of hallucinations, or else I was dreaming, but this perception was almost immediately forgotten in my helpless surrender to new and more vivid photisms, with an increasingly marked contrast between a sombre background and intensely bright light piercing numerous narrow apertures. The sombre surroundings altered scarcely at all: an endlessly ascending spiral staircase, wooden platforms, covered walkways where loose boards jumped under my feet, and octagonal 'round' towers. But everywhere at eye level there were dazzling chinks of sunlight in the dark walls: simple vertical or cruciform slits and circular or semi-circular dream-holes. Through these, when I looked out, I saw hazy and glaring industrial landscapes, areas of dereliction, waste ground covered with fireweed, with here and there an old building — school, pub, chapel — surviving in stark isolation, and also hoardings, railway sidings, spoil-heaps, cooling-towers, brown rivers and huge cuboidal factories with serpentine fire-escapes. By contrast, whenever he brought the 'sights' in his visor to the slits in the *bretêche* (the slits he called *arbalestinas*), or to the large loop-holes in the bartizan (the holes he called *canonnières*), the Man in the Iron Mask would report seeing the blue Mediterranean and jagged rocks far below. (This confirmed the general sense I had that we were supposed to be in Richelieu's fortress rebuilt by Vauban on the Lérins.) As the stairs twisted and we climbed even higher, the prisoner reported sightings of fishing boats and larger vessels in the Bay of Cannes. He mentioned the Croisette Point, and various strongholds, zig-zag fortifications, fortalices, walled towns, bastions and ravelins on the mainland. In the far distance, he informed me, he could see the snowy peaks of the Maritime Alps. He also commented on the continuous bubbling of doves all about us, in the walls, in the rafters above our heads, while I could hear a low continuous powerful hum that suggested heavy machinery, with shrill, rasping interruptions that suggested lathes, power-drills, motor-cycles. All this time the prisoner led the way, his close-helm now dull, now gleaming, while his keeper, the governor, meekly followed, a stranger in his own fortress-prison — every part of it completely unknown to him. We inspected no cells, we barely glanced into oubliettes, we discovered no suitable locutory. But we did open a large wall cupboard in a passageway. It was empty. Moth-haunted. And briefly we did look down a hollow shaft heaped with carrion that had been cats and dogs where each animal was impaled with a spike. We encountered no other human beings — no prisoners, no gaolers, no officers and guard on their counter-round, no watchmen, no sentries. When I woke, recovered my senses, or what you will, it was to find myself in Rampick's 'Bastille' garret, completely alone, the room empty of furniture and uncarpeted. I was standing before the dormer window that overlooked grey, drizzly Blackhorse Terrace. The earlier bright and dark violent sky was now uniformly dull. Coffee-coloured smoke from a chimney across the way drifted downwards aslant towards a street-lamp on the corner. I stretched out to touch the cold window-pane. I waited for reality to prove itself or for dream to resume its sovereignty.

CHAPTER SEVENTEEN

As I gazed out of the window I had a momentary impression of a figure in the doorway to my right, almost out of range of vision. A brown-skinned girl. Gypsy or mulatress. Perhaps merely the impression of a face, a smile. Sloe-eyes. Snub nose. Brown cheeks unusually high and broad. (How many words it takes to describe an apparition!) When she vanished, the girl's lazy, responsive, knowing smile, beginning as a gleam of new awareness, a mischievous gleam in the black eyes, was starting to spread downwards to the rest of the face, disturbing the perfect matt surface of smooth flesh over the hugely spheroid malar bones. My immediate thought was of La Voisin's sensual, cunning, gypsy-looking daughter, the girl starved or strangled three centuries ago at Belle Isle. Turned succubus. A dusky smiling beckoning spirit of the house.

I went over to the empty doorway and looked down the stairs. To the right, on this top landing, a short curving passage ended where the ceiling made an abrupt descent to the floor. Next to the attic room there was another door (ajar) that I had overlooked on previous visits. The fact that the door had a sneck rather than a knob suggested a cupboard. A closet. And so it proved. In one part this closet was lofty enough for a man to stand upright though the steep angle of the roof ensured that an upright stance would only be possible if he remained in one position just inside the door. I noticed a bulb. My fingers found the light switch but the electricity had been turned off. On a shelf a few candles. A hammer hung from a nail. Then I saw a parcel which I brought out on to the landing to investigate. The parcel contained a shirt, a pair of velvet knee-breeches and a sheath-knife.

I returned the bundle to the closet. Back in the dormer bedroom, in the centre of the bare room, a kitchen knife had been planted in the floor between two floorboards. So awed and frightened was I by the inexplicably sudden appearance of the knife (from that moment my state of mind was a strange mixture of lethargy and trepidation) that I felt I had no alternative but to take possession of it for my protection.

Downstairs the twin of the knife I held had materialized on top of the boxed-in electricity meter. I struggled in vain to open the front door. It must have been locked from outside. Through the letter flap I thought I recognized the Rampicks' next door neighbour. The man, having seen me, was retreating rapidly, apparently in alarm, down the steps to the pavement.

As it seemed impossible to make my exit that way, my obvious course was to leave by the back door. But I felt totally incapable at that moment of taking swift decisive action. Instead, a knife in each hand, I inspected the ground-floor rooms. I also listened at the foot of the stairs. At last I moved to the kitchen and the back door, laying the knives down on the draining-board while I struggled with three bolts and a large rusty key. The key eventually turned. The vertical bolts pulled down fairly easily. But the horizontal bar had to be worked across slowly with savage jerks.

Next, as carefully as possible (considering the state of my nerves) I wiped my fingerprints from the handles of the two knives. I congratulated myself on my forethought but every moment I looked about me and listened, feeling vulnerable because of my impaired hearing. I heard nothing until a woman's voice behind me sharply called my name.

By a miracle, when she spoke, I happened to be gripping one of the knives (wrapped in my handkerchief) firmly by the haft. I turned to face the intruder. An ideal 'mad knifeman' image in her viewfinder. (Her voice: argute, sibilant, I had recognized at once.) I came forward with the knife — not murderously, an instinctive movement. The shutter clicked. Instinctively I recoiled as the flash blinded me. In spite of the flash I had been able to see that Rampick's so rational unhistrionic sister was wearing a mask — something Rampick himself had never done. I was far too slow off the mark to catch her as she fled to the front door with her prize. The door slammed. I heard the key turn in the lock. A scrap of black cloth and elastic was posted through the letter flap on to the mat.

Yet another charade. A victory for the crone. (Provided the picture had turned out successfully.)

Her tactics had been flexible and daring. Part careful planning. Part improvisation as circumstances favoured. Perhaps she had overdone the knives. Had the mask been worn for her own protection? To give me pause? To make me hesitate in the event of my reacting out of character, quickly and with violence? I could not decide. A knife attack, causing bodily harm, would have furnished her with even more conclusive evidence than a photograph. And I had no doubts that Miss Rampick was capable of risking personal injury (even sacrificing her life) for the sake of her brother.

Still, with the estate agent and the neighbour able to testify to my presence that day at Blackhorse Terrace, and with the incriminating snapshot in her possession — if she had been lucky and I had not moved too suddenly or been too close — she would have convincing enough proof of my homicidal tendencies to persuade the authorities to reconsider their verdict on her brother. (Who could argue with a genuine photograph, unquestionably a true exposure of a mad knife-man, naked blade in hand?)

The trap had been sprung. '*The beast was in its toils*'.

One thing occurred to me. No matter how cunning and resourceful I believed Miss Rampick to be, she could not have stage-managed my recent hallucinations. Unless I had un-wittingly spoken aloud? And to take advantage of that she would need to have had the devilish foresight and the means to have filled the house with sophisticated 'bugging' devices. No, at least my hallucinations could not be used as evidence against me — as long as I kept silent.

After this bizarre incident I somehow composed myself. Self-consciously I walked out of the back gate into the cobbled humpbacked ginnel as though out on to a stage. Every moment expecting to walk into the arms of the Law, I set out for the railway station. Still at liberty I waited almost an hour for a train on the down platform, the only traveller seated on the only open-air bench. (In such an exposed position it seemed

tantamount to giving myself up.) On the train I slumped
against the window. It seemed inevitable that there would be
burly figures in uniform waiting at the barrier for my return.
And yet nothing happened. At the bus stop I was cursed with
the company of a large 'rotating' woman. She turned regularly
through an angle of 180 degrees, including me and everything
behind me in the sweep of her large round spectacles. But
neither then nor later was I accosted and taken off into custody.

So sure had I been that I would be arrested immediately that
during the following days, in reaction, I felt secure. Re-
assuringly I was undisturbed by visitors. I had no phone calls
apart from wrong numbers. In fact to begin with I slept for
twenty-four hours with only a couple of brief awakenings. And
subsequently I spent more hours asleep than awake. Deep and
dreamless sleep, except for brief dreams on the third or fourth
night. One of these concerned Brenda. The other concerned the
Man in the Iron Mask. In this dream I was scrutinizing a
postcard. The message (in Sylvia Rampick's hand) was: *Fouquet
arriving from the Ile Ste-Marguerite wearing an iron mask.* On the
reverse of the card I expected to see a photograph of the
prisoner's arrival at the Bastille. Immediately (in the dream) I
was ashamed at my simplicity. And yet now, as I write, I have a
distinct image of a tinted postcard view to accompany the
verbal description of his arrival. The prisoner in embroidered
justaucorps and wearing his polished close helm approaches a
drawbridge on foot under guard. Perhaps, after all, it did derive
from another dream.

On the fourth or fifth day Miss Rampick's letter came. The
postmark was almost illegible. Not a blackmailer's letter. No
reference at all to her stratagems, her newly-acquired evidence
against me. However this time she did urge me to give the
authorities a true version of the nature of the relationship
between myself and her brother and a true account of the
incidents that had led to my injuries in the old building. Her
stated reason for writing to me again was the rapidly deteriorat-
ing condition of Philip in the mental home. Reading between
the lines, of course, was the existence of the lever (which might
for all I knew have turned out less incriminating than she had

hoped) — the photograph she had taken of me brandishing a knife.

The same day I wrote my confession. I addressed it to Inspector Dixon but with only the vaguest sense that I was writing to a particular person. The general content of the letter was as follows. I wished to confess that in the old mill, on the night I had been attacked, I had provoked Rampick by threatening him with a knife. I had been incensed by the allegations he had just made about the morals of my estranged wife. Later, while I was momentarily distracted and fatigued, Rampick had attacked me in order to make his escape. My threatening behaviour must have made him fear for his life.

I followed the first draft with several corrected copies all tending towards the police-report English the headmaster long ago had decided was my characteristic style. I appended, as my reason for writing, the hackneyed formula 'to ease my troubled conscience'. I edited out of my final confession a couple of sentences explaining that my former misleading account was partly attributable to loss of memory. In fact this new statement was almost as far from the truth as my previous testimony had been. But what, after all, is 'the whole truth' in the public, legal context?

The fact that I could not assist the Rampicks in proving that the brother was innocent of the earlier attack on the youth made it all the more likely that the only result of my confession would be to damage myself, and lead to a fine, a term of imprisonment for perjury, or compulsory psychiatric treatment. But this last, after all, was the revenge the Rampicks had planned for.

I wrote with wearisome slowness, as self-consciously as if the Rampicks were looking over my shoulder. I read through each completed draft silently yet with excessively precise articulation, with longer and longer pauses between words. To make matters worse, while I composed these drafts, I was assailed and confused by the verbigeration of an autonomous external speaker languidly reciting a succession of proverb-type sentences (but with the stresses all misplaced) which I felt presaged at the very least a fainting fit if not a seizure.

The same day (or the next) I was found in a steep street in the neighbourhood of Blackhorse Terrace, lying half on the flag-stones half on the setts. I am told (I have no recollection of this) that when a woman asked me what the matter was I answered that I was looking for 'the gastar bubbles of yesteryear'. I was taken into custody as drunk and disorderly, for a time asserting argumentatively without variation (again I have no memory of it) that Balzhazzar was the son of Nebuchadnezzar.

I was later transferred to the Infirmary for observation and tests.

CHAPTER EIGHTEEN

Belcredi, one of the characters in Pirandello's *Henry IV*, cries out: 'My God, my God, madness is catching!' (or something to that effect). By this time I was ready to believe that such fears were perfectly justified. Madness *was* catching and could be caught even from a charlatan, a professional wits-stealer.

And yet I had to admit there was still the doubt whether a sane man could become mad by contagion, the doubt in my own case whether the sound man was *fundamentally* sound. Was it not arguable that I was already so out of sympathy with reality (irksome routines, myopic duties, all the wearisome *tracasseries*) that I could no longer be classified as sane? For a time I looked rosily upon madness as simply freedom from accepting the limitations of the quotidian. I regarded the fear of it as merely the fear of social ostracism, a shrinking from exposing oneself to the contempt the majority shows to the exception.

Would the castaway fear madness on his desert island? If the chief (perhaps the only) scourge of madness was the stigma attached to people in that condition, and the geographical solitary was consequently untroubled by this, should the prisoner dread madness either — immured as he was in his fortress-prison with no fear of repatriation to everyday living? I am conscious, as I write, of the non-sequiturs in my reasoning, but this was how I reasoned.

A good many of my preoccupations at this time absorbed me as though I had become the masked prisoner myself. For instance, for days I was preoccupied by thoughts of the vulnerability of the fort on the island of Sainte-Marguerite. My interest in this question was far more personal and intense than if it had merely been of historical or even authorial interest. At times I agonized, at times I exulted over the prospect of the fall of the starfort in the Bay of Cannes. Was there not always the possibility that the fortress might fall again to France's enemies as it had done in the days of Richelieu? Did the possibility never disturb the King? Was the prisoner recalled to Paris because such an eventuality seemed imminent? After much reflection I recalled Louis's instructions to kill the prisoner if discovery of his identity were threatened.

Another example. At one time I was preoccupied by the question of the Spanish Succession. My indignation knew no bounds that belated justice had not been done to the sacrificed twin and the throne given to another Philippe, the grandson of Louis.

I acted at this time as though I believed, or half-believed, that I was the masked prisoner. Somehow (gradually or by some trickery, a *coup de théâtre*) I had come to believe that an exchange of personnel had taken place. To be specific: between Rampick and myself. We had exchanged roles. (Note that at no time did I lose sight completely of the actors in the roles portrayed.) If I had taken over the role of the prisoner that meant that Rampick had become Saint-Mars . . . and the King . . . and d'Artagnan . . . and even the poor Scotch fellow Seldon . . . whoever he felt like portraying. As the role of the protagonist was immutable, indivisible and our cast was woefully deficient in numbers, the actor playing the deuteragonist should ideally be infinitely protean, capable of impersonating all the other characters. As occasion demanded. The whole of mankind theoretically. At least the masculine half. A role (roles) far more suited to Rampick than to me. As regards the weaker sex, in this particular closet-drama women were of very minor significance. If necessary the crone and the naked mulatress, *Mors* and *Peccatum*, could be represented by lay figures.

I had not, however, the advantage of Rampick's actual presence. And in fact I never saw Rampick or his sister again. I could get as far as setting the scene: a conventional dungeon, a garret, etc. I could bring Rampick on to the stage. But in my imagination his performance was incredibly listless, perfunctory. He entered. He sat down immediately as though exhausted. He muttered. He smiled wearily. He 'me-mowed' in my direction. He never took the initiative, content to wait and react to whatever I said. And then it was only to react minimally, with no conviction, in an uninspired, automatic fashion. In a strong light he was paper thin, transparent. Alone, although discouraged, I struggled on. To achieve verisimilitude I concentrated on the discomforts of the mask, the unbearable chafing of the iron headpiece, which I described as worse than the worst toothache. I struggled to bring the role to life by imagining and expressing verbally the pain, the various centres of pain downwards from the forehead and temples to the jawbone encaged in its iron *mentonière*, a freakish artificial mandible that exaggerated, that parodied cretinously, the movements of the lower face involved in speaking and eating.

All the time I was aware that I was merely recapitulating, without his flair, material from Rampick's Man in the Iron Mask diary. It seemed as if everything I said, everything I thought, were borrowed from a single source. According to Dr Scullard it was my disillusionment with a debased second-hand role that saved my reason. At this period the balance of my mind was unquestionably disturbed. I experienced no sense of freedom, no euphoria. On the contrary I suffered an abundance of mental torments, torments I hadn't bargained for.

It seemed that my desire to be confined at the safe centre of a series of concentric circles, an impregnable circumvallation protecting a cherished core of awareness, *although* an important aspect of my personality, was not the whole truth about me. Dr Scullard drew an analogy with someone who declares fervently and sincerely his love of solitude. (Perhaps, in the case of a great poet, he becomes famous as the Poet of Solitude.) Yet in spite of this quite genuine expression of a yearning for a solitary existence the same man has never been able to endure a day or even a few hours completely alone.

At this time, I made a number of drawings for Dr Scullard: actually little more than doodles in ball-pen. Only rarely did these succeed in representing even partially what I intended so I was compelled to add verbal clarification.

At the moment I can recall three of these drawings. All of them were sketches of the Man in the Iron Mask.

144

One was a skeleton, seated, the iron mask on the floor between his wide-apart legs. A skeleton hand rested on each femur not quite reaching the patella. In another drawing the prisoner (not a skeleton) wore a lantern instead of the iron mask. The most memorable drawing and the least successful in execution (far beyond my artistic capabilities) was a portrait of the prisoner with his mask removed. The head thus revealed, given the talent to match the idea, should have looked as if it had been flayed or scorched, a quivering jelly of raw, swollen bloody flesh. No doubt I was influenced by the popular misconception (as a child I shared this) that the iron mask was an instrument of torture like the Nun or Scavenger's Daughter! In addition to my verbal description of this portrait, on the same sheet I reproduced a supposed memorandum from Louis XIV to Saint-Mars in which he had written: *'When no likeness to my own or to any human face remains, then and only then have you my full authority to remove permanently the iron carapace from the head of the state prisoner, Dauger.'*

I hadn't expected to make a friend of a psychiatrist at my time of life. Very quickly my initial wariness, hostility even, had changed to an attitude not far short of slavish submission. I assented to the rightness of all Dr Scullard's opinions and diagnoses. In general he gave me to understand that I was abnormal chiefly in being unduly susceptible to influence. And *that* to a large extent was due to the unhealthily solitary life I had led since my wife moved out, to my continually morbid state of mind. There was no morbidity to compare with the morbidity of the sexually deprived, especially where the fact of deprivation was not even admitted and was confused with religious fervours and crises, the torments attending imaginary transgression, unreal scruples. He referred to the lives of several great Victorian celibates who had confused religion and sex.

In my case it was not just a matter of sex. And not at all a matter of religion. But social deprivation he said could be equally crucial. My appetite for social experience, for companionship, was small. I was deficient in the ability to organize my leisure time. Most men deserted by their wives would have had a greater range of occupations and satisfactions available to them (even apart from a liaison with another woman) — supportive reassuring routines they could turn to at a local public house or social club, the golf course, the regular ritual of spectator sport. He was surprised that I watched so little television — it would have fitted so well with my depressive conformist passive personality. He laughed at my explanation that since Brenda had left me I had never been able to get a reasonable picture on my television set. When asked to name my favourite television programme, the romantic, chauvinistic 'Flashing Blade' came to my lips (the often repeated French swashbuckling serial dealing with the siege at Casale). My hesitation, my subsequent embarrassed disclosure of the name of a children's serial (which Dr Scullard was clearly not familiar with and doubtless believed to be only suitable for young children) seemed partly to amuse, partly to exasperate him.

Dr Scullard was fond of literary allusions and analogies. He invited me to think of the protagonist of the typical classic ghost or horror story. He listed the salient characteristics. A celibate. A man (or woman) abnormally lacking in close family ties. By nature rather cold, anyway deeply repressed. Nervous. Sensitive. Vulnerable. Educated but without means. With little or no sexual experience. A bachelor curate. A lonely student or scholar. An anaemic copying clerk. An isolated governess.

'This is the sort of person,' he continued 'who is particularly prone to see visions, to surrender to an eerie atmosphere, to give credence to the power of irrational forces.'

From my own reading did I not agree?

In such stories it was always the fastidious, diffident man, the solitary precisian, who had systematically recoiled from close physical relationships with anyone, who was destined to be the man marked out for a terrible fate, an intimate, uniquely intimate contact with the inexpressibly loathsome, the un-namably perverse repulsive Horror.

'The psychology of such stories is perfectly accurate,' Dr Scullard maintained. 'Only the claptrap, the evasions, the hyperbole of the everlasting "nameless horrors", the '"unimaginables" and "indescribables" reduce many of them to bathos. At bottom even the most naive reader knows very well that the indescribable horror is a clumsy analogue to the basic sexual experience the hero has overwhelmingly feared and desired.'

In a spirit of raillery, he went on to inform me that I reminded him of that redoubtable duo, the academic virgins Miss Moberly and Miss Jourdain, who persuaded themselves they had seen ghosts at Versailles, out of an overpowering need to relieve the monotony of their circumspect lives. My own cosy 'adventure' was to swallow with amazing gullibility first the idea that my neighbour could be consistently adhering to a role he had adapted from legend and literature and to believe (or very nearly believe) that he could be living in another dimension in which he actually was the Man in the Iron Mask.

'You will only be cured,' he told me. 'when you are thoroughly disgusted with the banality of your threadbare conceit.'

Dr Scullard showed remarkably little interest in the fate of Rampick. When he was released I was not informed. (Perhaps so as not to worry me.) The ultimate fate of both Rampick and his sister I learned by chance from a newspaper. When I brought the cutting to Dr Scullard, he told me he already knew all about it. He also told me that he did not wish to discuss it — even though the circumstances were so unusual, so strikingly apposite. I interpreted the doctor's unusual reticence as being part of a deliberate policy to 'demythologize' the figure that had unsettled my reason.

CHAPTER NINETEEN

Rampick and his sister had both drowned. Their bodies had been found in the river estuary, on an outlying shelf of rock near the site of a fort. At some time in the past I had seen this fort from the opposite shore. I had at first assumed it was as much a part of the gimcrackery of the outmoded and downgraded holiday resort as the hardboard 'castle gates' entrance to the pleasure-beach, or the forlorn naked gammerstang of the condemned iron pier. Later, however, I had read somewhere that in spite of its inanely conventional resemblance to a gigantic sand-castle the fortress walls had been built of a particularly adamant stone and cemented with a liquid volcanic substance that over the years had grown harder than the stone itself.

All my efforts of retrospection added nothing to this scrap of local knowledge, a memory less reliable than the tiniest, most faded and urochrome old snap, a single titbit of information gleaned who knew where and exactly when?

The newspaper account did not say how close to the fort the bodies had been found. Bangbeggar Sound was mentioned (I found this on a map) and also the name of an unpretentious seaside town (not the nearest) where the couple had been staying. There was a reference to 'mental trouble' which hinted at suicide. The analogy between the English fort and the French fort on the island of Sainte-Marguerite I had been eager to discuss with Dr Scullard. Clearly he did not care to discuss it.

It was this attitude that for a long time decided me against showing him Rampick's postcard. The postcard had arrived the day after I learned of the fatal accident — 'a message from beyond the grave' that I was not going to sacrifice lightly. (I felt there was a real danger that Dr Scullard might tear the card in pieces before my eyes.)

Instead I undertook the journey by rail and ferry to the scene of the drowning. From a curious sightseer I overheard directions that took me to the precise spot where the bodies had been recovered.

However, as I stood before the huge brackish expanse of water I did not have any sense at all that the site of the drowning had been localized. It is not to be supposed that I stood alone at the edge of the ocean. On a semi-circle of concrete already invaded by weeds and backed by willow herb cars and a hot dogs van were parked. There were numerous relics of past visitors — cans, chip trays, cartons — inside the graffiti-scrawled bus shelter, in the car park, and on the muddy fore-shore where gulls swooped and screamed. For a long time the only real thought that entered my head was to wonder why seabirds were so much less piercingly vocal on ponds and reservoirs inland. I felt strained and impatient and suffered from a headache just above the eyes. (It was an overcast and yet, at times, a glary day — a day of dingy brightness.) I was excessively anxious about how much time remained before the next ferry. I had forgotten to wear my watch.

How could Rampick have confused these murky heaving waters with the warm azure of the Mediterranean? The Lérins, belatedly fortified, had seen assault, recapture. By contrast two World Wars had passed by this battery commanding the neck of a broadening river, protecting the approaches to a major port. This new item of information was derived from an old man, a native. Amazingly he had seen 'the man who drowned himself'. He was not romancing. He described to me Rampick's long raincoat, his fussy mincing walk and the hard-faced woman, his companion.

'You could tell he was mad just by looking at him,' the man told me. His tone expressed no sympathy at all with the insane.

'Did he make any enquiries about the fort?' I asked, having wrongly jumped to the conclusion that the man had spoken to Rampick. I received a startled look and no audible reply.

Yet when I asked him if he believed the drowning could have been an accident, he stated plainly his opinion that the wife (*sic*) had probably tried to save the fellow from himself and had perished with him in the attempt — a theory I had also entertained but without precisely formulating it. In other respects the man revealed no signs of special percipience, complaining of the litter and recalling the old days.

Posthumous feelings. Perhaps if I wrote 'The Rampicks are dead. I am alive' a thousand times. . . .

Yet I can't imagine them as corpses. I imagine them still alive on their holiday — the distinguished, frail Rampick, shoulders bowed, in his long overcoat that looked like an apron, almost a soutane, his wiry plain virilescent sister in her wide, corded skirt, firm and erect on her lark legs.

Strange that during their lifetimes I had never once seen them together out of doors and now in my imagination I see them always together, on the muddy foreshore near the old fort and the old lighthouse.

The picture postcard that I was afraid Dr Scullard might confiscate out of exasperation was not a view of the sealed-off pier or the Napoleonic fort but a lurid, vulgar joke card depicting a weedy rabbit-faced youth—cyclist with puncture— and, confidently astride her machine, his nubile companion, boyish of face, with scarlet pippin cheeks and short corn-yellow hair, her vigorous femininity concentrated in the golden glabrous thighs, in the twin cannon-balls that surged out very high beneath her sweater's turtle neck.

On the back of the card Rampick had written an odd assortment of taunts about the more ridiculous aspects of my 'servile personality', 'a limpet derelict living off the taxpayer'. It ended with the words: 'I cognosce you an imbecile.'

Altogether it resembled no card I had ever received, disparagement of myself forming the whole content, the style exclamatory, forcible-feeble, the vocabulary inflated, recherché, perhaps a parody of what he considered my style to be like. The card avoided giving any information about himself or his sister.

When I finally decided to show the card to Dr Scullard (by which time I had received a second card more than a fortnight later and a third a few days after that), his ironic comment was something about deadwood — driftwood — drifting to the shore — a reference, of course, to Rampick's name. Recently Dr Scullard had got into the surely reprehensible habit of referring to him as 'the Rampick'. This seemed to me in incredibly bad taste considering that the man we had both known was so recently dead.

He pointed out similarities between the handwriting (in his view disguised) and my own hand — which I emphatically denied. He seemed disinclined to argue. I had to press him to take account of the postmark, the date. Did he believe I was making regular journeys to the coast to post these cards to myself? He pointed to his 'ls', and 'hs' and most obviously the 'ss' on the first card. According to him these were basically the same as the characters I wrote. It was self-evident and would not deceive a child. Was it not far more likely, he declared, that I was writing and posting the cards to myself than that a drowned man was sending them to me?

'What if they are not dead,' I countered, 'and this is their final attempt to persecute and drive me mad?'

But unfortunately I had mislaid postcards two and three and could not produce them when Dr Scullard, with a marked lack of enthusiasm, asked to see them. The more assiduously I turned out my pockets the more sceptical and weary grew the expression in the psychiatrist's eyes. Then, looking grave, he wrote a prescription for new tablets.

On my way back to the flats I did something completely out of character. When a fawn mongrel, appearing from nowhere, almost tripped me before running on to a concrete lamp-standard, I rushed after it. (It had only just lifted its leg against the post.) And in a spirit of revenge, or at least with the intention of administering a sharp rebuke, I smacked its prominent rump. The dog turned, snarled briefly and snatched at thin air in lieu of my hand before making off, watering the ground as it went, across cindery waste land.

Shortly afterwards, as soon as I found myself in the forecourt of Ruskin House, it was extraordinary the amount of deference I was shown by everyone — neighbours, distant acquaintances, complete strangers — the sort of deference normally paid to royalty. The doors of the building were opened for me by a working man in a dark suit and white shirt buttoned to the throat without a tie. A man I had once wrongly suspected of being too friendly with Brenda. He smiled deferentially while, feeling rather faint, I rested leaning against the door before proceeding to the foot of the stairs. I thanked him for his courtesy with a bow. I would have made the bow much lower had I not been feeling so exhausted and out of sorts. Even back indoors, when I crossed to the window, a number of people standing motionless, singly or in twos in doorways, on the grass, on the paths, were looking up as if waiting to catch a glimpse of me. All had the same expression, the same posture that expressed deference, concern, a genuine interest in my welfare that was neither impertinent nor hypocritically obsequious. It was a rare fustigation I had given the biscuit-stealer! I recognized him down there among his fellow citizens. Yet apparently he bore no grudge; he quietly observed me with the same humble, sorrowful, tender concern as all the others.

I felt so faint that almost immediately I was forced to lie down on my cot from which position I could only see the sky and, in an oval mirror across the room, glimpse a scrap of salmon-coloured tile and the burnished cone of a turret across the courtyard. I had never before imagined the world could be so full of goodness, of an agreeable subservience about which there was nothing servile, nothing slavish.

What had happened to transform these people, the beastly burgesses of yesterday?

In my saner moments, when I read over what I have written lately (when I am not, for example, obsessed with the moral dimensions and political consequences of the decision made by the ruthless Cardinal, the weak King, and the callous Queen, in respect of the succession and the twin princes) what strikes me most is the meanness of tone of the 'sane passages' and the much more exalted and satisfying tone of madness. In recent weeks Dr Scullard has been far less sympathetic to my writing.

He discourages me at every opportunity and would probably like to destroy these pages. It is fortunate for me that such a course would seem contrary to medical ethics. One day Dr Scullard said bluntly that he considered very little of my manuscript would survive if some sure touchstone of truth could be applied to it. They say that a wicked book is all the wickeder because it cannot repent. The fictional d'Artagnan of 1700 spoke of a book he knew (the Bible) which never lied *as so many others did*. The 'fictional' d'Artagnan, mark, so sensitive about the truth! The fact that these words were imagined by the arch-fabricator, Courtilz de Sandras, makes it a very rich irony. Of all the hundreds of untruths embedded in the text of his *Memoirs of d'Artagnan* the most outrageous must surely be the allusion to King Louis as ' a hero of the first rank'. But who is to say what are straightforward lies and what barbed, vengeful ironies savoured in his solitude by the hounded, imprisoned author adventurer?

Nowadays I am not encouraged to speak to Rampick or his sister. Not now that they inhabit the same dubious shadowy regions as the eclipsed sun King and his masked prisoner. It seems the dead immediately lose all relevance, all significance to the practising psychiatrist. Dr Scullard concerns himself exclusively with the living, the observable.

CHAPTER TWENTY

All my life the new has appeared to me in the guise of the strange and fearsome — never as the exciting and challenging. New routines. New scenes. New people. A thorough change the doctor prescribed. Salutiferous Monkwell: overcrowded, harsh, antiquated Monkwell! For ten weeks the deranged and their keepers, my new companions.

The official reason for my incarceration was that it was more practicable to treat me there under observation and in groups with other patients. The reason for my release (my own speculation) was that Dr Scullard (a most unpopular figure, by the way, to the inmates) can no longer conceive of a day when I am either totally sane or virtually cured and only likely to have a relapse once a year . . . I almost wrote on Bastille day . . . but the nineteenth day of the eleventh month would be even more appropriate.

Compared to the treatment of voluntary outpatients, the treatment given to residential patients (I speak from my ten weeks' experience of Monkwell) is more direct, more informal. The tone is harsher. And not only the tone. But speaking of tone, since my release, simply from the inflexion of Dr Scullard's voice when he says, 'And how are you?' it is plain that my condition is a matter of small concern to him. An efficient doctor (cost effective) he knows when to cut his losses. Evidently also my case had lost its novelty.

To her credit Brenda was at first reluctant to cooperate with the doctor. What finally persuaded her were the two occasions when I addressed her as 'Countess' and condemned her roundly for her cruelty in imitating the limp of kind, good natured Louise de la Vallière. It is a fact that when I addressed her thus she was limping. Other explanations, however, might have occurred to me. Perhaps she had been beaten by an uncouth pimp she had mistaken for *a cavaliere — servente*. And if that were true, what a scandal that the modern counterpart to witty, vivacious Olympe Mancini should be treated as degradingly as Basinière's whore! Having written that, it troubles me that 'Basinière' may not be the correct name. Is it not rather the name of a prison tower I mentioned earlier?

No Rampick to help me over details like that.

No longer.

Not since he decided to drown himself in the vicinity of what must be the only structure within a hundred miles that by any stretch of the imagination could serve as a passable substitute for the meridional fortress of his dreams.

On my second visit there I had climbed to the ramparts and observed ranks of seagulls drawn up before the bastions on the vast wet sands. In phalanxes, as if for review. At Monkwell, in my imagination, I went for frequent morning or evening strolls along those ramparts. Unspeakably satisfying to isolate myself on those remote fortifications. To strive manfully with the elements in the rain and tempest. And at night, during a brief respite from the shouts of a recalcitrant inmate, if I concentrated with my inward ear I could distinguish the surge of the tide from the snapping of an old pennon and the ghostly echoes of bugles.

At Monkwell (no more sordid than most such places though obviously one to avoid if at all possible) there was an unexpected bonus: an angel in mortal guise. This was a mature woman with natural blonde hair, an august brow, miraculously youthful milk-white skin, perfect exanimate features — no, not 'exanimate', for if they expressed nothing else, those features expressed innate pride, pride of caste, pride in her virtue, an unconscious superiority to all the other patients (and staff), a saint among sinners. . . .

I have forgotten what I meant to say. There was a woman at Monkwell, a woman I associated (in appearance only) with my own conception of Louise de la Vallière. Pride of caste. Pride of chastity. But unlike the morally frail, though uncharacteristically finger-grained and in certain respects scrupulous concubine of history, this was a Louise with truly exceptional standards of virtue. I cannot believe that even the most devoted and the most ardent admirer had ever been permitted to kiss as much as her fingertips. Do I need to assert that this saint among women would have been incapable of debasing herself by consorting with anointed human filth on the loftiest dung-heap in the land? This 'Louise' (her real name was unworthy of her) I was convinced would make her final devotions as a nun, a vestal whose austere outmoded vocation was somewhat mocked by her voluptuous curves, the generosity of her physical endowments. But how appropriate (especially in the twentieth century) that such a woman should be found languishing in a madhouse. A devastating reflection on the times that it seems perfectly natural, only to be expected, that a beautiful virgin of mature years should be a lunatic.

By contrast how much closer to the preferred lifestyle and aspirations of millions is a woman like my wife. A soap-opera heroine. A wholehearted votary of lechery with an attractive personality, a refreshing candour, a beguiling impudence. In an earlier age I could imagine her acquiring riches and territorial titles, prizes won — by her animation, daring opportunism, and statuesque *and* flexile body, at the cost of a little perspiration, consistent counterfeit ecstasies, regular cheerful parturition — from the inflamed sceptres of princes. Famous, incidentally, for a head-dress or hairstyle, *Fontanges* or *Pompadour*.

I am glad that I was not present at the fall of my ideal. I heard her screams, not dreaming it was her.

I learned about this later. The only person in the place I spoke to regularly told me what had happened. It was towards the end of my stay there that I became friendly with this man, who had become briefly notorious when he was prosecuted for setting fire to all his firm's paperwork. It was discovered that he performed this public service several times previously, using a variety of aliases in various minor official posts in both private and public organizations. It was always in a state of rapture that he had set fire to the records of his employers — rapture, he emphasized, not strain, not harassment, not overwork as anyone might reasonably have supposed. Usually we got along well together. Within limits, as I shall explain, we pretended to take an interest in each other's obsessions. However, since it is a fact (as I think Rousseau once observed) that an eccentric, original man rarely has any genuine, durable sympathy with the crotchets and fancies of an individual of comparable eccentricity (your peculiarities are not my peculiarities) we practised an uncommon and dangerous kind of honesty which involved each of us in openly declaring when the other had become or threatened to become particularly irksome — as I am afraid I did all too frequently. As soon as I referred to the woman I associated with Mlle de la Vallière ('that chalk-faced woman' he said of her, 'the bad case of *la belle indifférence*') his eyes would glaze over and if I was foolhardy enough to embark at length on the subject of the masked prisoner, or (as I had a mania for doing at that time) on the lawless amours of the masked prisoner's brother, the supreme cock of that golden dungmere of a court where the only females to escape the royal puissance were the impregnable nymphs and goddesses scattered about the groves, he would beg me to stop, saying that he had never believed that virtue should be its own dismal reward and that listening to me strike the same note a thousand times without flinching must make him elegible for a pension not to say a canonization. A man of intelligence, he was fluent (unlike Rampick) in spoken and written French but showed no sign of interest in French history or culture. He thought I was terribly *borné* with my constant harping on the court of Louis XIV and the Man in the Iron Mask, the latter a topic serious historians had long ago lost any respect for. He even cast doubt on the independent existence of Rampick, whom he considered a mere mouthpiece, a conversational device, a mirror image. I promised myself that I would arrange a meeting with Dr Scullard to make him eat his words. Before this was possible his incendiary tendencies were revived. On the day I was released he was still incommunicado in a refractory ward.

I have various theories about the reason for my release. Perhaps it was simply that my basic normality became more apparent in those surroundings. Or perhaps it was seen that the company of mad people was bad for me. Certainly from the time of my arrival until my departure from Monkwell I had a sense that the place was in perpetual masquerade; that individuals who had turned themselves into mountebanks, dancing dwarfs, clownish peasants, were acting deliberately, provocatively, in their chosen roles to confuse and intimidate their fellows. This made me behave, in turn, with what I considered to be impeccable moderation. My extreme circumspection was only equalled by the majestic reserve, the serene impassiveness of the beautiful blonde quasi-nun. She, unfortunately, was repressing with only temporary success the simmering violence within her.

Back in my own flat I was agreeably surprised that everything seemed very bright and in reasonable condition, especially in the living-room. Fortunately I knew how deceptive appearances can be and so I was not too surprised or disappointed when within a few days I had become familiar again with the pock-marked skirting boards, the grime of the lace curtains, the window-sill graveyards for flies, moths and beetles, the furfuration that whitens the sloping shoulders of the wooden 'thirties' clock, the grease-marks visible on the pale spines of certain books.

The condition of my bookshelves, my usual cosmic hopeless-ness, a ball-bearing-sized lump on my back, and the clutter in the drawer of my writing-desk (not used any more for writing since the flap was broken), are the first excuses that spring to mind to make sense of my decision to forfeit the rewards of old age. And my 'despair' at the sight of an untidy drawer is not intended to be as flippant as it must sound.

The terrible disorder in the drawer normally does not trouble me — not while the drawer is unopened. But immediately after it has been closed, while the memory of the disorder is vivid to me, it is unbearable. I keep opening and closing the drawer as though to convince myself it is not, after all, too bad or to get accustomed to the sight which does not help. The reverse, in fact. It makes me physically ill that this drawer, that so many hings in the world, are, or can at any time become, so disordered, beyond my (and the world's) energies to put to rights. This anguish at potential as well as actual disorder I realize is ludicrous, as also is the assumption that I am incapable of tidying and straightening anything, even one drawer.

I have always felt incapable of repairing or making things. This helplessness has extended to almost all areas of daily activity and since I was at Monkwell my capacity to cope seems reduced even further. What I do still accomplish I have to rush at full tilt before I lose my nerve.

I have already made arrangements for my 'day of indifference'. As well as the tablets, I have bought a bottle of whisky. I will leave this unopened until the 19th November. I have even written the customary letters (none of this seems real) well in advance. A letter to Brenda begins 'Our (I have underlined the Our) divorce is now absolute.' I have bequeathed (by letter) my part-typewritten manuscript in its large spring-back binder to Dr Scullard. I have no very sanguine hopes that it will win belated appreciation in that quarter. Who else could I leave it to? My wife?

I have a tendency at the moment to break down in tears, an unpromising state of mind for someone considering making a success of his 'day of indifference!' This unmanning tearfulness began the day I returned to the flats and saw 'Loony Phil' written on the landing wall. It was written in the angle by the door where I could not fail to see it. So far I have not been jeered at in the streets. In my absence the flat had not been broken into. Isolated in the dust of the living-room table lies the goosequill attached by several narrow rubber bands gyved round and round a ball-pen. Goosequill! Companion of my lucubrations! Not the same ball-pen that I started out with but the same dusty feather still in reasonable trim. When I sit facing the faded letters of the old hatter's slogan, the wall (the bastion of Sainte Marguerite), the pigeons, the occasional herring-gull, my ball-pen quill, and the rickety card-table, all remind me of days of comparative pleasure, even hope.

If I were to write now 'the rest is silence' . . . (what Barbellions of disappointment and injured pride are concentrated in that phrase!) . . . you are not to assume that 'silence' neces sarily refers to the silence of eternity. Encouraging concept though that is. (By the way I hear at full volume once again the uproar in the forecourt.) There is considerable interval between today and the 19th November. Who is to say if my resolution will last until then?

It discourages me already that I cannot achieve the same admirable symmetry as the poet Mahalin who, obsessed like me, seized the opportunity presented by the two-hundredth anniversary of the unknown prisoner's death. What kind of anniversary will this year be? On the other hand it is possible to argue that one should have fewer pangs about quitting such an undistinguished year and decade. On a note like that (jejune, facetious as it is) I almost feel like concluding.

This manuscript was given to me by Sylvia Raistrick, widow of the late Philip Raistrick. Apart from writing this note I have merely added the obvious title 'Man in the Iron Mask'. As his doctor and friend I am in a position to confirm that Philip Raistrick had been obsessed by the legend of the masked prisoner for a considerable period of time. Philip did in fact take his own life on the day and month indicated at the close of his narrative, in 1969.

A. F. Menzies, MA, MD, FRCP